ALSO BY ELIZABETH ROSNER

The Speed of Light

Blue Nude

Blue Nude

A Novel

ELIZABETH ROSNER

Ballantine Books
New York

Published in the United States by Ballantine Books, an imprint of The Random House Publishing Group, a division of Random House, Inc., New York.

BALLANTINE and colophon are registered trademarks of Random House, Inc.

LIBRARY OF CONGRESS CATALOGING-IN-PUBLICATION DATA
Rosner, Elizabeth.
    Blue nude : a novel / Elizabeth Rosner.—1st ed.
      p.   cm.
    ISBN 0-345-44222-9 (alk. paper)
      1. Germans—California—Fiction.   2. Israelis—
California—Fiction.   3. Artists' models—Fiction.
4. California—Fiction.   5. Artists—Fiction.   I. Title.
PS3618.O845B58 2006
813'.6—dc22   2005052410

Printed in the United States of America on acid-free paper

www.ballantinebooks.com

9 8 7 6 5 4 3 2 1

FIRST EDITION

for Puro, with love

Prologue

He could have been lost. There was no moon and his eyes had adjusted to the darkness and there seemed to be nothing but wheat fields in every direction, low hills on one side and a forest in the distance ahead of him, but nothing that could be considered a landmark, nothing familiar. His compass had been stolen, along with his jacket and his watch, all pulled from beneath his head so carefully he hadn't awakened. But his gun was still in his hands, and he gripped it harder for reassurance. He must have been lying on it with his fingers locked so tightly that whoever stole his jacket didn't dare try to take the gun too.

The moon would have helped. But then again, light of any kind would have exposed him too, and maybe it was best to have the cover of darkness until he found his bearings. Maybe he needed the dark for his own protection. Enemy lines shifted so quickly sometimes that for all he knew he was at this very moment not the occupier but the prey. For all he knew.

A barn made itself visible against the dark field on his right, a barn that was so shadowed it might have been imaginary. Except the closer he came, the more he could make out the silvery gleam of its faded wood, the reassuring bulk of its roof and walls. Closer still, he picked up wind-wafted scents of hay and manure. Somewhere nearby there was livestock, cows maybe, or horses, though probably not pigs because he would have recognized them from his childhood summers on his grand-parents' farm.

That was a world away. Some other time and place, a dream to him now. Before he knew what it meant to point a weapon at a human target and pull the trigger. Before he knew what dead bodies looked like, the eerie absence in their staring eyes, their gaping mouths and tangled limbs.

He tried not to think as he walked closer to the barn, tried only to strain his eyes against the night and listen for the sound of anything moving, test the air for the smell of danger. He tried to become animal and leave his mind out of it.

That was how he had learned to keep firing at the line of bodies standing along the edge of a ditch. To leave his mind out of it. To aim and fire, again and again. Not him doing it, not even his will, just the tension and release of his muscles, the trained machine of his body.

The house on the far side of the barn was empty; somehow he could tell this from its loose-hanging shutters and broken win-dow beside the front door. Some family had fled, or something worse. It wasn't the house that interested him, though; it was the barn. There was warmth inside, an abandoned animal per-haps. Mostly, he imagined it would be a place to sleep. Even a pile of hay would be safer than where he had been.

A human-sized side door appeared more beckoning than the larger main doors, and he felt relief when it opened quietly. He tried not to breathe much, tried to enter in near silence while he sniffed the air for signs of life, peered into the black-ness as if he might detect ghosts.

Nothing? Almost.

There was a scent he was sure was human.

He froze, and listened, gripping the hard steel of the weapon in his hands.

Something was definitely alive in there. Amid the odors of hay and dung and dust and moldering wood, he could make out a human smell too, and not his own. Without being able to see, he felt his other senses compensating, and he listened hard until he found it: the sound of someone breathing.

Who is it, he said, making his voice deep and, he hoped, threatening. Who's there.

Nothing answered, of course, but he wanted them to know he knew. He wanted them to know they were found out.

He pointed his gun into the space before him, turning right and left with it. You see? he said, even though he couldn't see anything himself.

I won't use it if you come and show yourself, he said. Come where I can see you.

Nothing again, although the breathing was still there. Someone trying not to be heard, but not quite inaudible.

I'll wait until morning, he said, though he knew that would mean more hours without sleeping, more hours in the dark. At least it would be warm. Slowly he moved away from the door and into a corner, leaning his back against the walls. Waiting.

The light, when it came, was gray and then pink, revealing rafters and a ladder to a loft, hay stacked in piles and also strewn. He could see the gleaming edge of a metal bucket and a pitchfork stabbed into some hay. But no signs of life.

All right, he said, clearing his throat. Had he slept? He hoped not. I can dig for you, he said. Or you can just come out.

When he heard rustling overhead, from the loft, he pointed his gun in the direction of the thing emerging and stepped closer to the bottom of the ladder. It was a woman, or maybe even a girl—he wasn't sure yet. She was pulling hay from her clothes and her hair, speaking in a language he didn't understand. Maybe she was saying Please. Her eyes were so wide they made her appear feral.

With his gun still aimed at her, he watched her raise her hands in the air over her head and crouch down until she was kneeling. Her skin was as pale as the moon and her mouth was still forming words he couldn't understand. She was no more than twenty, probably even younger; her face was streaked with dirt, and her lips looked chapped from thirst or fear or both.

He was supposed to shoot her; that was clear. It was what he had been doing for weeks now, shooting people who looked more or less just like her, older, younger, all of them praying or begging for mercy, all of them lined up at the edge of ditches they had dug themselves, and he was not supposed to hesitate at a moment like this, no questions to be asking. This was the machine's job, after all. His weapon was cold and heavy; he felt himself aching with the effort of holding it.

Her face went paler still, until her eyes looked like holes in the night sky. She bit her lip until it bled a little; she seemed almost like porcelain to him, and yet those smudges of dirt on her face reminded him that she was real and alone and far from everything familiar.

His gun pulled at his muscles and his knees were locked, but still he didn't make a move to pull the trigger. These people were lower than animals: this was what he'd been taught—that they were nothing to him. But meanwhile, here he was, wishing he could speak her language, whatever it was. Wanting to know her name. Needing all the blood washed from his hands.

It was as if the war left his body and he was empty of it. The gun weighed so much that he had to lower it; he had to let it drop all the way to the ground, his fingers relaxing for the first time in weeks. He wanted to fall to his knees the way she was; he wanted to collapse in surrender and deliverance.

He looked at her beauty and could not look away.

Part One

The Present

Chapter One

BEGIN ANYWHERE, Danzig says. The shoulder, the rib cage, the thigh, the ankle. It won't be an accident, even if it feels that way right now.

He stands in his classroom at the Art Institute, the students arranged on chairs and stools in a rough circle with their sketchpads and charcoal, all sixteen of them waiting for the model to take the first pose on her platform.

Find a place where your line wants to take a journey, he says. Some curve in any direction, a place where skin meets light, meets shadow. Let your hand tell you. Begin there.

It's almost the last class of the semester, and he is deliberately talking about beginnings, not endings. He keeps promising himself he is never coming back, but he keeps coming back. For the third year in a row, he has made a vow not to return in the fall, but he's finding it hard to take his own word seriously. Even when he is shouting at his students, feverish to convince them to care more, he feels his own intensity in doubt, wonders how much he still cares himself. He used to relish the moments when they jumped at the sound of his voice, but now he is no longer sure that anyone even flinches. Their anonymous, hopeful faces may not be enough to save him.

On the worst days, he feels that he must be getting old and used up. The youngest students who pass him in the hallways barely seem to acknowledge he is alive. To them he might as well have one foot in the grave.

But wait. At fifty-eight he can still attract plenty of attention when he wants to. It's just a few of the women, girls really, who infuriate him with their disinterest.

HE STANDS BESIDE his faithful skeleton, the one that dangles like a marionette on its wooden stand, its bleached bones as familiar to him as an old friend. This is the invaluable prop he calls Doctor Memento, for *memento mori*, though Danzig is sure most of the students imagine he must be referring only to his own death and not theirs; they're so young they are still convinced of their immortality.

He is not allowed to touch the models; that's one of the rules of the Models Guild. And so instead Danzig will rest a hand on Doctor Memento's shoulder blade, tap a fingertip on his collarbone. Today, he casually holds the good Doctor's left hand as a form of mild entertainment or even consolation. Later, he will gesticulate with its digits for emphasis, always reminding the students to keep track of the bones.

Look closely, he tells the students. Deeper. This is the predictable architecture of the body. This is how you pay attention to the truth.

Twenty fresh faces arrive in his class each semester, young men and women with barely tolerable moods and attitudes, startling shades of dyed hair and ubiquitous piercings. Fifteen weeks ago there were twenty of them, and now there are sixteen. Though he used to be able to predict with surprising accuracy which of them would leave, this semester there are more stubborn ones than he had counted on, furiously scratching at their sketchpads.

It takes a few weeks or sometimes just a few hours before he knows whether or not anyone in the room has talent. In the first few meetings they are blurry and indistinguishable to him. Now, he sees that several are frowning or grimacing, already prepared to be dissatisfied with the first gestures on the page, already wanting to tear sheets away and throw them aside.

He admits with a private sigh that there is not a single student who engages him right now. For a long time, the opposite happened, and a student would get under his skin by being infuriatingly incompetent. There was one girl last year whose drawings were always filled with oversized, unmatched hands, lopsided mouths, heads shaped like eggs or apples, eyes too high or too low.

You're just not looking, he had growled at her. Do you mean to tell me these hands belong to the same person? You're not even trying.

He knew she probably hated him, his icicle heart, his mouth twisting and cruel. She thought he was a mean bastard, and she was right. He was. She left the class and never came back.

They seem younger than ever, these students, almost another species. He swears to himself he was never that young, never that naively arrogant. On certain days there might be one or two who remind him of those first Americans he met, all those years ago. The Occupiers, his father had called them. Soldiers. But he has mostly forgotten.

Begin again, he says.

SOME YOUNG WOMAN with peroxide hair about an inch long and a silver stud through her tongue (she is yawning, even now) seems to be glaring at him. More likely she is angry at the world, but Danzig takes it personally, so he is angry at her too. In the past he would have managed to seduce her after the first or second week of the semester, just to wipe the glare off her face. But this is what outrages him as much as anything: she doesn't seem to register him in any way as a sexual being. She turns her back almost every time he passes near her.

He might have reassured himself with the certainty that she doesn't like men at all, but in fact he's seen her more than once with her pierced tongue in the mouth of a leather-encased, acne-scarred boyfriend, who drops her off and picks her up on his motorcycle.

So it's just Danzig who doesn't appeal to her. All that sexual heat and none of it for him.

He tells himself he doesn't mind, not about her or about any of the rest of them. He has made no promises and told no lies. And he is about to forget each one of their names.

TODAY'S MODEL is getting undressed behind a folding screen. So far he can only see the back of her head, noting very dark brown hair, cut in a kind of thick bob above her jawline, wind-blown and messy. There have been so many models—easily hundreds over the years, possibly as many as a thousand—so many whose names he cannot remember and probably never knew.

Just last week his model hadn't shown up at all, and Danzig had posed for the class himself, stripped down to his jeans and bare feet, determined not to squander anyone's time including his own. He is still vain enough to know that his muscle tone is reasonable, his back and shoulders powerful enough to be compelling anatomically.

The students could work with a piece of clothing for once; it wouldn't kill them, he said. And here was a chance to practice contours half hidden under fabric, folds and creases and what they used to call drapery in the days when nude models were rare and for men only.

He used a long stick kept on hand for prying open and closing the high casement windows of the room. He held it like a staff of Moses, aimed it like a javelin, used it to prop his arms like a weary shepherd. He imagined himself through their eyes: his blond hair going gray at the temples and on his exposed chest, his charcoal-stained fingers. Rocking almost imperceptibly on the balls of his feet, he reminded himself to bend his knees, all of this giving him a renewed appreciation for the balanced stillness of his models.

All of the students seemed to work especially seriously that day, a little shy of him at first and then with increasing eagerness, obviously hopeful in the face of his silence that this might be a once-only chance to work without his correcting hand hovering nearby. For now Danzig's hands were elsewhere, held in a foreign gesture that had nothing to do with their own hands, except that it had everything to do with getting his hands to look as real and as still as the ones they saw when they looked up from their easels.

There.

He was there for them to study all they wanted, a body twice their age at least, maybe three times, and suddenly a figure in space with a look that might have surprised them had any of them been curious enough to decipher it carefully. He felt vulnerable, subject to a persistent gaze that made him worry about what they thought of him, whether the young women saw him as old and unattractive, past his prime; whether the young men saw him as weaker than they'd ever allow themselves to be, a man without much of a future, a father figure who needed, basically, to step aside so that the youth and promise they held could stride ahead and take over the world.

BEGIN AGAIN, he says today, even before the model has stepped onto the platform.

It's not just a beginning every time you see a new model, he continues, but every time you face a fresh page. It's that necessary leap into the unknown. And even though you know you're compressing the infinite possibilities that exist just before the first line is made, you still have to make a commitment. It's a direction that can be changed even when it declares itself to be irrevocable.

They look at him, at least a handful of them still willing to hang on his every word. There are several, he knows, who stopped listening weeks ago. They draw and fail and draw the same thing all over again. They're like dogs with bones, stubborn and single-minded.

It's their loss, he thinks, but never mind. They'll end up where they started, with or without me. If I'd really wanted to be one of those eternally patient fathers I would have stayed with Andrea and raised the child where I could have some say. Never mind.

Still holding up Doctor Memento's left hand to point it at them, he looks at nothing for a few silent moments, feeling a low hum of expectation and anxiety in the air. Maybe a few of them really are afraid of him, as if he is the enemy, not the work itself.

The day he modeled for the class, he thought he overheard someone refer to him as The Kaiser. The comment was low and muttered somewhere behind his back. He was caught so completely off guard that he barely admitted his own shock; it was too absurd. He would have expected worse, in fact, but they didn't know anything about their own country, much less about the rest of the world. All they recognized was his blond hair and blue eyes, his imagined lineage on display. But he brushed it off.

What did they know? he asked himself. What could they possibly know?

YOU CAN NEVER HOPE to be able to finish a painting unless you truly know how to start, he says. Unless you're willing to practice that first movement over and over. To turn seeing into a stroke.

He gestures with his arm, moving it like a swimmer, and the arm of Doctor Memento moves too.

Stroke, he says. Learn how to pull yourself through the water. Feel the pure balance between tension and release, the arm loose and strong at the same time, finding exactly where the angle works best. Part the water as if you could divide it into Before and After.

The model steps out from behind the screen and looks at him neutrally, with apparent calm, though her gaze is aimed just past him, over his shoulder.

She is lovely, he thinks, not beautiful in the usual boring ways. There is something else.

He does his quick, expert appraisal. Dimensions, he thinks; that's what she has. Space between her features, her breasts, long arms and legs and torso. Smooth unblemished skin, those very dark eyes, a full mouth, even without a smile. Her fingers are long and tapered, and she is completely unadorned. No makeup or jewelry or tattoos. Just a pure unveiled being.

He says what he always tells the models: that he wants her to start the session with twenty one-minute poses, and up she steps onto the platform.

What he will remember later is that Billie Holiday was playing, that the light pouring through the high windows was diffuse and fog-colored, that as far as he could tell none of the students truly realized just how good she was, from the moment of her first pose until the unraveling of the last one.

He will remember pacing back and forth between the platform and his skeleton, taking its hand and dropping it, taking it back again. For the first time in all his years of teaching he barely notices himself talking about bones, about the need to remind them what the body is made of, the mathematics of anatomy, the beauty underneath beauty.

He can only see her.

Chapter Two

BEFORE TAKING her first pose, before stepping into her stillness, Merav is struck by the image of a man holding hands with a skeleton. It's a startling first impression, captured only in her peripheral vision, yet one she will not forget.

But of course this is a life drawing class. He is teaching the lessons she has heard so many times before, not only during modeling sessions but in classes when she was a student herself: the proportional rules for hands and feet, the number of points where bones are visible under the skin, the practice of seeing the gestural line at the center of a pose.

Now the instructor has dropped the skeleton's hand and left it swinging slightly. Walking toward the platform, he announces her first series of poses, and Merav feels sixteen pairs of eyes following the map he traces, searching her body for corresponding clues. The students measure her, counting distances. They hold up their twigs of charcoal the way he has undoubtedly shown them, marking their way down the length and breadth of her body. At his cue, she turns like a dancer on a music box. She takes steps in slow motion, as if underwater.

Walking is controlled falling, he says. The center of gravity is shifted ahead of the base of support in the direction the body is moving. Look.

One of the instructor's hands is reaching toward her back but doesn't touch it. She imagines she can feel the tense muscles of the students as they watch, their eagerness to do everything he says.

Find reference points, he tells them. And use them. The head is a reference for the shoulders, the breasts. They become reference points for hips, thighs.

He aims the tip of a pencil at her, gestures back at the skeleton.

Everything is connected. You draw the head and forget it! You draw the arms and forget them! No. You're drawing a whole figure, something unified. If you want to draw a monster, fine; draw a monster. But if you want to draw a body, draw it whole.

Fleetingly, almost as though she has been touched by a ghost, Merav sees an image of herself in a black-and-white photo, one taken by her ex-husband. It is a portrait of her legs, from hip to heel, illuminated by natural light and free of context, disembodied and afloat in space. She had arched her back and leaned out of the frame; her arms were over her head holding on to a bar attached to a wall in Gabe's studio.

Mostly, he didn't title his photographs. But that one he did, naming it after one of Paul Klee's drawings: *Angel Brings the Desired.*

The teacher's voice brings her back again to the present. Merav's friend Lucy, the one who got her this job, told her she thought his name was Danzig. Lucy pronounced it as if she didn't know it was the old name of a now-Polish city, and Merav didn't correct her.

He came here from Austria, Lucy added. That's what everyone says.

What else do you know about him? Merav asked.

Well, he's famous from way back for some big gloomy paintings, Lucy told her. And he's pretty abrasive. Most people actually consider him a son of a bitch, she said, laughing. I guess the best you can say is that he can be a little hard to take sometimes.

Now that Merav is here in the room with him, she knows he's not Austrian but German. It is unmistakable, that accent. She has no doubt. Having listened to accents all her life, and known how to recognize the tongues of so many places, she trusts her ear.

For those first several moments, she isn't sure she can manage to stay in the room. She's stunned by this almost primal response, her coiled readiness for flight. But of course she stays. She steadies her heartbeat, calms herself down. She is experienced, a professional. She will do her work, and he will never know how the sound of his voice threatens to expose her far more deeply than she feels now in her nakedness.

Still, her body finds its own way to speak.

BETWEEN POSES she breathes deeply to let the music fill her with a kind of liquid peace. Billie Holiday. A pure melodic line pours through her bones, allowing her own lines to find their song. Merav composes herself in the air the way she imagines a composer makes music, the way poets build stanzas.

Sometimes Danzig stands at his own easel, a piece of charcoal in his hand. He keeps his eyes on her, as if his hands need no particular attention, and he brushes his page with lines briefer than his words.

You can render completion with simple strokes, he says. You can imply everything.

Something about the way he moves his arm when he reaches for his drawings, something about the way he scrapes at the page, makes her feel like flinching. It's internal, her response; she is sure no one can see it. But it's almost as though he is touching her. As though he is leaving marks on her skin.

WHERE'S THE OTHER ONE? Danzig asks Merav during the first break.

She has wrapped herself in a faded red silk kimono and is resting in an old overstuffed chair, the same one every model probably wants to collapse into during breaks. But Merav keeps her back straight even when she's sitting down. Pulling one knee to her chest, she absent-mindedly massages her calf muscles, rolling her head to loosen her neck.

You mean Lucy?

Yes, Lucy. He appears careful not to stand too close to her. She is guessing he has repeatedly been warned away by so many others. All those rules about space.

She couldn't make it, Merav says. Told me she had a migraine headache.

Merav doesn't want to tell him she's not on the list, that Lucy called her instead of the Guild for a replacement. She's been hoping he would not ask. The people in the Institute's office don't even know she's here. The paycheck will go to Lucy, who will pass the money along to her.

Danzig seems to ignore the students filing out the door,

already fumbling for their cigarettes. Not a single one stays behind to continue working through the break; that's what Merav notices.

You're very good, he says to her. His voice sounds both serious and deliberately offhand. She thinks he is watching now to see whether she'll blush or look embarrassed, but she simply nods and lowers her gaze. She can't help noticing the vivid light in his pale eyes, but she doesn't look directly at him, not yet.

Thank you, she says.

In her bag there is a water bottle, a thermos of tea and an oat scone, all of which she begins to dig for. She doesn't want to be rude, but this is her break time, a chance to sit quietly and rest everything, including her concentration. She would like to be alone in the room while they all go outside, including this German man.

The scone is in pieces, which she takes one at a time into her mouth, breathing deeply. While she poses she has to keep her breath shallow, and now it feels like bliss to be able to fill her lungs and sigh all the way to empty.

I didn't get your name, Danzig says.

She sips her tea, says it as softly as she can without being rude, and is utterly relieved when he doesn't ask her to repeat it.

I'll talk with you later, he says. All right?

Merav nods her head again. If she doesn't say much, she thinks, maybe he won't recognize her accent the way she has deciphered his.

LATER, TONIGHT, when she's falling asleep and reviewing her day, she will remember the way her body reacted to his voice. The poses she took in the first session were all in the shape of fear: a woman turning away from something threatening; a body in flight; the curled-up shape of self-defense, protecting the heart, the belly. She said nothing, but her body spoke its own language.

Chapter Three

OUTSIDE, THE SMOKING STUDENTS lower their voices when Danzig opens the door to the patio. He smoked too, for decades, along with every other artist he knew. And then, four years ago, he stopped. His doctor had threatened him with such ferocity he had actually decided to quit. Like that. Occasionally, the seductive smell of it will beckon to him, but today he's in no mood for being tempted. At least not by his students' cigarettes.

He's not interested in summoning them back inside, but they seem to think that's what he's there for. Reluctantly, they interrupt their brief pleasure as if that is what he expects them to do. Smudged with charcoal, happily marked by their signs of willingness to get dirty for art's sake, the students offer him wary sideways glances. Even the angry girl seems calmer now, loosened by her nicotine daydream.

Black hands, forearms, streaks on their foreheads and elbows and clothing. They have the pallor and stains of coal miners descending into the earth. Digging for vision. They are trying so hard, Danzig thinks.

And then he notices the way the sun bounces against the concrete with so much intensity. Here we go all over again, he almost says out loud. Summer is approaching and with it the chasm and the abyss, the opportunity and the terror. He has been on this threshold so many times, nearing the end of the school year.

Following the students back inside, half gazing at the back of the angry girl's bleach-tipped head, he is struck by how slender her neck is, how it seems so insubstantial for a task as critical as holding up her skull.

Anatomy and desire, bones and terror.

Mournfully aware of how much he wants another cup of coffee, Danzig names what he holds in his gut: fierceness, pleasure, and something that he is sure is a new kind of exhaustion. If not this, he tells himself, he'd be enslaved by some gallery, painting the same paintings over and over and pretending that he wasn't. He'd still be caught in the foolish riptide of his longing for fame, dragged under where there was no air. This is his escape, or part of it anyway.

It's just that instead of pushing his body to the edge of collapse, painting into the late night, filling himself with fumes and wine and smearing everything in his world with splotches of oil—instead of all that, he is pouring his passions into these students, giving them whatever he can afford to give away.

It's yet another way of leaving himself behind in the world, another way of creating. Or at least this is what he tries to believe.

A steady paycheck from the Institute means that if he doesn't want to paint, he doesn't have to. He has known so many painters who lost themselves in the pursuit of money, a gallery or a manager always pushing—either for more of the same, which was death, or for something they considered

newer and more exciting than the last piece, which was another kind of death because it meant someone else was telling them when to change directions or where to go in search
of something.

And when it came from someone else it meant the painter
had to carry around some question about whether that voice
could be satisfied. Danzig knows that the only voice he needs
to satisfy is his own, and that is elusive enough.

THE STUDENTS SHUFFLE BACK into their seats, some of them
agreeing to change places, as if they still haven't understood
that the model is going to keep offering them new angles.
Danzig stands once more at his easel, the music descending
into brief silence before starting up again.

He will call her M., since that's all he really heard of her
name, and all he can remember. She is back on the platform,
inside a pose.

Danzig tries to make sure he has no recollection of this
model stored somewhere among the few truly memorable
models he has seen over the years. There was that one with
the only tattoo he ever really appreciated—an open lotus
flower at the small of her back. And another one with an
astonishingly pronounced rib cage—she was a dancer, and
much too thin, but he was amazed at being able to see such a
detailed version of those curved bones making a cage for her
heart and lungs.

There have been men too, of course, athletic and well-
defined or paunchy and tilting toward decrepitude, older than
himself and even more of a *memento mori* than his skeleton.

There were the lean young dancers, male versions of the ballerinas with eating disorders though perhaps not quite as slender, and with a similar freedom in their limbs as though not quite bound to the earth.

More than enough of them had what could be described as beautiful bodies, flawless even, but of the ones good enough for his students—the ones who weren't always inspiring but at least were useful enough for anatomy practice—he was always searching for that unusual stillness, an awareness of negative space, an ability to design lines that could be treated from anywhere in the room.

A set of muscles in the back or the thighs, a particularly lovely pair of breasts or arms, a melancholy in the face. It could be anything. He always knew when he found it.

And of course there was Andrea, and there was Susan. He sometimes forgets they had once been models, since they had so fully become something else.

LOOK AT THE PULL of gravity on her face, Danzig says, because he can feel that the students are expecting him once again to say something.

It's second nature to him, this art of seeing the intimate gesture embedded in the posed body, the line that determines everything else. Can he really teach them how to find it? Especially when it vanishes so quickly. A couple of heartbeats long, a breath or two; his hand has to move without thought pushing it; his hand has to arc across the page before there is even time to send it. Everything else is remembering.

Study where the right elbow fades into the knee, he says.

They still don't know. He has to help them find the single line as it constantly turns and explains the form, turns and explains, all along its journey.

Begin again, he says.

Chapter Four

ONE OF THE STUDENTS, a young woman with dark eyes and long brown hair pulled into a loose knot, reminds Merav of herself six years ago. She used to sit in the corner too, strands of escaping hair always in need of attention, her sketchpad like a shield against any distractions.

So much concentration and longing. Merav recognizes herself even in the way this girl (somehow she seems like a girl) chews at the corner of her mouth, squints at the sketches in her collection, appears completely unhappy about all of them.

Merav always thought her drawings should have been better, should have reflected more of the perfect arrangements she saw when she studied the models. Just out of the army, in art school in Tel Aviv, Merav felt caught halfway between proficiency and disaster. She couldn't seem to find her own voice in her fingertips, couldn't stop comparing her own work with that of the other students in the class. Everyone else seemed more talented or at least more sure of themselves, more willing to assert their lines and shadows on the page.

Then one day, everything shifted when the model failed to appear for the life drawing class. At first, of course, there was collective concern for her safety. When people missed ap-

pointments, even when they were unusually late for something casual, the unspoken fear was that something had happened, an accident or worse. This was what they lived with
all the time. This was why phone calls were both terrifying
and reassuring. No one knew what kind of news was on its
way.

Still, the instructor was increasingly frustrated at being
stood up; the class was restless and distracted. Merav surprised herself by making her offer with almost no hesitation.
Even in retrospect, she couldn't quite name where her impulse had come from, although there were so many possibilities. Curiosity. A desire to risk losing her anonymity. Some
hope that she might discover a new life inside her own skin.

Many of her classmates told her afterwards how amazed
they were, how it was nothing they had considered for even
a moment. Not out of modesty or embarrassment, but just
because they didn't think about it.

There were models and there were artists, they said. You
were either one or the other.

When Merav offered to pose, Professor Cohen seemed
caught off guard for just a moment, though clearly pleased.
She was tall and black-haired and strikingly angular, a former dancer who still walked with an unmistakable ballerina
turnout. Merav was fairly sure Cohen had been a model herself at some point, so maybe that was why she had been so
encouraging.

It's an excellent experience, she said to Merav. Even if it's
just for the one time. You'll learn something about yourself,
and about how the body works. Go ahead.

Merav went into the small bathroom in one corner of the
classroom and removed her clothes. When she came back out

and stepped onto the platform, she was nervous, her skin prickling. It wasn't her own nakedness that seemed strange, but the fact of being the only unclothed one while everyone else stayed safely hidden.

A warm breeze touched her from an open window, and somehow that soothed her, rinsed her a little. When Professor Cohen asked her for the first pose, Merav closed her eyes for a moment, then gazed hard at the ceiling. Somehow, amazingly, her body knew what to do. By the end of the third pose she felt she was another person.

Merav is a natural, someone in the class said quietly. She couldn't tell who it was because he was somewhere out of her range of vision and she was holding herself very still. Maybe the voice was right. Maybe this was some ability she had possessed all along and didn't find until now.

She found places to rest her gaze: the patterns embedded in the stucco walls of the room, the shape of table legs, shadows on the ceiling. She stood and sat and reclined. She felt the seduction of sleep but resisted because she had to hold herself in place, keep her hands exactly where they were when she closed her eyes.

The fingers still. Zero at the bone.

Like the exhalation just before pulling the trigger. *Now.*

The same voice that said "Merav is a natural" said later, Look at that beautiful curve, the muscle along her rib cage when she twists like that. Do you see it? Just there.

He must have been pointing. Merav didn't hear an answer to his question, but she felt a kind of peace she had never felt before, as if she were some beautiful found vessel on an archeological dig in the desert.

This is my body, she thought.

She felt like a swallow, dipping and soaring at twilight. She felt her body touched without being touched.

MERAV BEGAN TO MODEL for some of the same art classes in which she had been a student the year before. The more often she worked, the more she learned how to listen to the signals of her muscles and bones. There were poses that couldn't be held for long, others into which she could settle and rest, be a pool with no ripples, water at the bottom of a well. What was essential to her was knowing where the pose felt right.

Now, six years later, she is amazed at how much she knew immediately, intrinsically—how much this feels like another form of art. Her body as a composition and an instrument.

For the quick gestures she doesn't even need a timer; she counts in her heart. For the long poses, she has to note the negative spaces, the areas outlined by a curving arm, a bent knee. She has to know how to find them again after a break so that the lines are uninterrupted, continuous, so that the artists can be returned to their trance.

It is a surprise, and yet it isn't: this discovery that she can picture herself through their eyes, that she can give them whatever they need. Anatomy is more than bones and muscles. Her body is an abstraction, a narrative designing itself in the air.

SOMETIMES WHEN SHE IS POSING, the teachers talk about Merav as about a collection of pieces. They say, The breasts are here, the hip bones come out like this; the arm is bending more at the elbow—and remember, it is hair, not a helmet. They say, The spine is not as straight as you've drawn it; the waist is fuller like this; the chin is pointing more to the side—and when are you going to start drawing hands and feet? What are you afraid of? It's just a body. Don't think.

Occasionally this disturbs her, the idea of being viewed so impersonally, of being so unseen even as she is gazed upon for hours. But that is the paradox. She is unveiled down to bare skin, exposed that far, but the world inside her body, the universe of dream and sensation that lives beneath her bones stays covered. All of that belongs only to her.

She has seen models take poses as if feeling their way in the dark, deciding in slow motion how far to reach a hand, where it might touch a wall or window. But her quiet certainty is her gift.

A twisting torso is more interesting than a plain stance; one leg bent is better than both legs symmetrical. Not that she has to consciously decide these things anymore. Her body knows its repertoire, though it is something different than repetition. Some models develop a set of poses like a choreographed routine and dance it over and over. But Merav knows she isn't just a figure for them to study; she is a character in a setting, an actress, a silent film.

Sometimes she uses props, fabric, costumes. A black slip, some old high heels with straps to leave undone. Kimonos, scarves, shawls. Thigh-high stockings. There is texture to feel against her skin and to give the students a little more to work with.

Sometimes she does a series of famous poses, or several from one artist, Manet's *Olympia*, Klimt's coiling nudes, Matisse's odalisques, Renoir's girls doing their hair. Sometimes a teacher asks for graceful, romantic poses: her pretty little self. Other times they don't want hands across her body, or they want no hands showing at all because fingers are hard for the beginners. Sometimes she has to stay symmetrical, or all closed up.

Mostly she immerses herself in the mood of her day. Anger, frustration, sorrow. It's a way to release feelings, to let go. And she gets paid for the time to think, time to daydream.

Long ago, she realized that the in-between stages of undressing and re-dressing had to be minimized. She was either clothed or nude, moving very quickly through the process of getting from one state to the other. These were the ordinary moments, the ones belonging to everyone else, and even though she believed art was also about the ordinary, sometimes, for her, it was not the point, not what her presence was about. Her intention was always to heighten what was real, to offer the gaze an invitation, to focus on something impossible to capture.

THE VERY FIRST TIME she posed in Tel Aviv, she didn't want to see the students' depictions of her. At the end of the class, she dressed quickly and left, vaguely aware of the chorus of gratitude that followed her out the door. She didn't know whether she would model again, but mostly she wanted some time to herself to think it over, to consider how it felt. Somehow she suspected that knowing too much about the effects of her posing would confuse her, or even upset her.

Hours afterward, reflecting, she realized she was actually afraid. She worried that their images would reveal her flaws, exaggerate her weaknesses, depict who she really was. She couldn't imagine yet what would happen when she allowed herself to see what they saw.

When she returned to class the following week, some of the students offered to show her their drawings, and she accepted reluctantly. There was her spine, the definition of its ridge and the shadowy valleys on either side, the twisting of her wrists and her head. She saw the shadows of her nipples, her pubic hair; she noted the arc of her jaw and the space between her eyes.

And then she heard an echo of her mother's voice saying, You're full-hipped and small-breasted, just like me. As if making sure Merav knew what category of body she belonged to.

She felt herself back inside the scene of her own fourteenth birthday, visiting her mother's apartment on the kibbutz so they could celebrate together with cake and tea. It was clear from the way Ilana frowned at herself in the mirror that her own body didn't please her; she sighed and tried to resign herself to what she had been given.

It could have been worse, she said, looking at Merav with commiserating sympathy.

The question of beauty, for her, was such an old one. It had begun with Ilana's mother, Esther; her stories about the war, about the Nazi occupation of her native Holland. Even after Esther's death, Ilana kept the story alive by repeating it.

First there was the wearing of stars, the flimsy yellow thing we had to sew onto our coats, Ilana recited. JOOD, it said. But if you were beautiful enough to pass for a non-Jew, you didn't have to wear your yellow star. You could walk on the sidewalk instead of the street; you didn't have to walk with your feet in the horse droppings but could be up higher with the other beautiful people. And this made such an impression on her. She was just a girl.

This was when Ilana would pause and wait for Merav to say, Yes, I can imagine it. Ilana must have had to say the same thing herself when Esther told those same stories before Merav was born.

The lesson continued. Esther was sent into hiding from the Nazis, paying a Dutch farmer with pieces of the family jewelry to keep her in his barn. And when a neighbor denounced them for hiding Jews, Esther's secret was revealed.

This was the moment, the one that lasted for the rest of her life. A young German soldier stood with his gun aimed at Esther's heart. She prayed it would be over quickly. But he looked at her with such pure admiration it was clear he couldn't kill her or even give her up.

He fell in love with her beauty, Ilana said, quoting her mother. He couldn't stand to point a gun at something so perfect, so lovely. And so he let her go.

NOW, STANDING IN THIS CLASSROOM with so many more of these depictions of her, more mirrors and reflections, Merav wonders all over again about beauty: her own, her mother's, her grandmother's too. She is still wondering what beauty is. Wondering who decides whether or not you possess it, whether or not it possesses you.

Is it true? she wonders. Can beauty save your life?

The German man's voice finds its way to her ear one more time. Begin again, he says.

Chapter Five

EACH MODEL IS UNIQUE, Danzig says, even as he points back toward Doctor Memento. Anatomically speaking, exactly human and exactly herself. Every shoulder blade conforms to the rules but also holds unique planes of light and shadow.

This is the moment. For you to say *Yes*, and *Now*. Do you see?

M. is a body turned away, shoulders and nape, one hip angled against the platform's cushions, a curve of buttock and small of back. Ribs. A column of spine, vertebrae articulated like buds on a branch, waiting to burst into life.

Nothing is ever accidental, he tells them. Even the white space is deliberate and accounted for, present because of an intricate relationship to the whole. Balance, harmony, unity. A sentence is a complete thought, expandable and reducible, yet self-contained.

M. could be too lean except she isn't, her flesh softening the lines but pressing the bone too, allowing Danzig to read her like a map. He is only partly stunned by the intensity of his desire to touch her. It has been a long time since a model pulled at him this way, skin looking as though it's made of light, an infinity of refraction making his eyes ache. A lunar light, the way the full moon appears as if it is the source of such illumination when we know it is only borrowing from

something else, measuring the distance from the sun, showing us that miraculous brightness.

He imagines this: cupping her breasts and testing their
weight in his hands to be sure they fit when his mind has already predicted it and his palms already tell him Yes. To
press himself against her, to fold themselves together seam
to seam, the way certain insects mate into one flying being.

He imagines them ascending.

The body exists in space, he says to the class. There is
something solid she is resting on; that shape is part of what
makes her stand the way she is standing; her feet are on the
ground, or she is sitting on a chair, or leaning against a wall,
or reclining on pillows. The body is a part of the world. Do
you see?

The CD changer makes its clicking windy noises as it re-
arranges the music. Billie Holiday has long ago given way to
Van Cliburn and now to Bob Dylan. He notices M.'s awareness of the music as if it were a score for a film. She seems
present inside her body, even as he senses she could be departing from it, or entirely absent.

That's a good chair, he continues. It holds her. There is a
weight to the body; the limbs have a direction. The hips are
tilting, but still there is solidity to the legs; they're holding
her up. The skeleton is a system of weights and balances; the
joints are there, the muscles, the torso resting on the bones of
the pelvis. The hip sockets tell the legs where they can and
cannot go.

Anatomy is what's possible: the limits of the body; and
gravity defines the intentions of the flesh, the pull downward to earth.

Do you see when she turns, how the ribs have to adjust,

how the weight in the knees changes? Are you looking? A body in motion, a body at rest—well, it's the illusion of rest, but that's what we do. We create illusions, because that's all we can do.

Danzig too is a body in motion while he teaches, hovering over a student at work, gesturing at the model and back at the skeleton. He always names the bones and muscles, even as he knows they aren't trying to remember.

See how I know them? he says, wanting them to bother. They take a separate class for anatomy, but he insists on making his point.

It's not just guesswork, he says. It's part of being good at something, the work of preparation. So that when I draw a line to represent the clavicle my hand knows exactly where to go.

He draws on the students' work sometimes, to make a line more emphatic, to show what it means to make something concave, to help them see what he means. They are too young to have any legitimate possessiveness toward their work; they need him to interfere. He is so much better than they are, so much more experienced at seeing. It's a way to awaken them, he thinks, to open their eyes, teach the hand a particular way of moving on the page.

Sometimes he has to resist the urge to push a student out of the way so the drawing can be taken over completely; there is so much wrong and so much he wants to change. They need his help. They will thank him for it later.

His own teachers were ruthless with interference, with control. His most significant teacher—the unforgettable one from all those years ago, Professor Hoffman—had even prevented them once from drawing while the model was in the room. Hoffman wanted them to devote themselves to the study of the body, to memorize it so fully that only after the model was gone, only then were they allowed to begin.

Last week, when his scheduled model didn't show up, Danzig actually considered doing that himself, forbidding them to draw while he was posing, then leaving the room while they worked. It was such a vivid memory: the beautiful dancer who had twirled for them, Hoffman telling her when to move and when to freeze, all of them spellbound as they watched her. No music, no distractions, just the body, her limbs extended as if pulled by invisible strings, the cords of her taut muscles, her face a quiet mask. Hoffman told them to sit on their hands if they had to, but warned that if anyone even tried to make one line on the page he would throw them out for good.

This was how he taught: like a military commander, as if they were soldiers in his private army. It was bizarre and often deeply unsettling: how much Hoffman reminded him of his father. But Danzig knew this was what he had come to the school to learn. He knew that somehow this discipline would be what set him free.

After half an hour, maybe more, the dancer grabbed her clothes and left the room. They sat in silence for several minutes, as if in shock, or in prayer.

And then they began to draw what she had left behind.

Hoffman had been the one who insisted that Danzig and his classmates use cadavers as models too, pushing them past their revulsion and fear toward what he demanded: a deep respect for the body, its mysteries and symmetries.

There is no substitute for this, he said. No stillness like the dead, no other chance to see what this vessel is really all about. When the spirit is inside, it is something else. But this is the only way to study form absolutely.

Something about Danzig posing himself last week brought back images of Hoffman that were so intensely vivid he lost track of time and let the class go well overtime. At one point he actually heard Hoffman's voice rumbling in his ear and had to shake himself free of his pose.

Don't look away, Hoffman had said. You must not look away.

WHEN M. TAKES HER SECOND BREAK, she wraps herself in her kimono and goes out into the hallway so quickly, blending so fully among the departing students, that Danzig loses sight of her completely.

The room is empty; the music is playing only for him. At the easel, his demonstration drawings beckon to him. He stares at the page from across the room, looks toward Doctor Memento as if the skeleton might have something to say.

But the voices are inside himself, filling him like old cigarette smoke, like stones.

Chapter Six

OUT IN THE HALLWAY, Merav searches for a drinking fountain so she can refill her water bottle. She drinks with her head tilted all the way back, water pouring down her throat as if clearing its way through a column of sand. This is the last break of the morning, the one when she usually feels the most tired and ready to stop, the one when she begins to imagine stepping down into a pool of water, liquefying her limbs. Soon.

It's what she does to rinse away a modeling session: either a long bath or a swim at her neighborhood pool—both if she has enough time. She heals her limbs this way, releases them even as she retains her quiet center point. The water is always about forgiveness, about reminding herself that she is whole and self-contained, an island. Submerged, she takes refuge from the gaze of others as if the water were a kind of cloak. Gone are the interpretations and revisions, the outlines and shadings. At rest and alone, she can hear her breath and her heartbeat, slow as a wave.

Still, swimming is paradox too: all the way here, in America, being in water helps her remember some of the most sensory qualities of the kibbutz, the textures of her early life she will always carry. The way the orange groves sent their fragrance into the air like an orchestra, the way the roosters

predicted the dawn. The way the pool looked just before anyone dove into it.

Only in water does Merav feel perfect in her skin. Clothing never fits easily: her body always seems to her either
bulky or constricted, weighed down or lost. In water she
breathes freely, as if her skin and lungs are all connected and
she finally has enough of the air she needs. Once, a painter
told her that in Chinese medicine it's believed the skin is an
organ, the largest organ of the body, and it breathes or has
trouble breathing just the way lungs do.

Sometimes Merav thinks that modeling is one of the
ways her physical life resembles that of her childhood on the
kibbutz. All the children used to run around without clothing, boys and girls together, swimming and bathing and playing. A great deal of time, it seemed, was spent in their
unself-conscious nakedness. That was why Yossi felt so much
like her animal mate, the boy she knew for so much of her
life that his body was almost as familiar as her own. By the
time they became teenaged lovers, she already knew perfectly well that they had the same skin color, the same shape
of eyes. Their hands were exactly matched, finger to finger.

A year older, Yossi wore his army uniform first, and she
thought it would feel a relief to follow him into the army too,
to join that larger family of young people all alike. But when
her turn came, the uniforms deeply disturbed her. Even
though the point at least in part was to reinforce that sense of
unity and sameness, for Merav there was also the shocking
disturbance of conformity. Suddenly she felt vulnerable, to
see that what she wore made her look like a soldier, like
everyone else, and so they were all interchangeable and re-

placeable. It scared her to be so generic, so much a part of the giant machinery of the country in which she lived.

What consoled her were the moments of open and ordinary nakedness, the locker rooms and showers, where for a while at least she felt all of them returning to their skins. Individual colors came back: their hair, their shapes, their breasts and thighs and backs, so much beauty and variety, one at a time and unique. Merav was allowed to remember what she really looked like.

Even after the army she had a confusing sense of what clothing was all about. At first she felt what all of the soldiers must have experienced: the odd transition back into civilian dress, the ability to choose what to wear every single day, whatever they wanted. It was exhilarating for a little while, and daunting too, to have so many choices, to have to decide all the time.

She realized with surprise that the uniforms had been a kind of blessing, something she did not have to think about, something that let her focus on other things. But there she was, paying attention to clothing all over again. Though for Merav it was new because on the kibbutz the clothing was so basic it never seemed to demand much notice.

IT WAS TWO YEARS AFTER she had completed her army service when Merav left for America, heading directly to San Francisco and her cousin Yael. Numb with grief, needing distance from everything familiar, she embraced the idea of living farthest from the place so many other generations had landed, those waves and waves before her.

Everyone said the new waves now were coming from the far western corners of the globe, so far west they became the east. Merav was from the Middle East—whatever that really meant, since all of it was relative to someone else's point of view. To herself, she was from the center of the world exactly, and heading to another place that eventually, she hoped, would feel like the center to her too.

She'd lived on the edge before, of course, the edge of a small country always in danger of obliteration, disappearing by the sheer will of its neighbors' hatred. At least that's what she had been told all her life: that her neighbors wanted death for her and everyone else she knew and loved.

It had happened to Yossi, as if to prove the inevitable.

And then she broke the code, leaving instead of staying, disappearing from view as if in defeat. It was the only way she knew how to save her own life.

AFTER MERAV'S FINAL POSE of the class, the one she has held for an hour, she goes behind the screen to climb back into her clothing. No one is talking. Some of the students are still looking at the place where she has been, studying her ghost image.

Sometimes she allows herself to imagine that in Israel, there is a ghostly version of herself too. An echo, a shadow, just like the one these students seem to be watching.

The German man has become quieter and more removed, which has been a relief. Now he is leaning against a far wall, watching the room, looking as if he might collapse if not for the wall holding him up. Merav doesn't catch his eye; she just reaches for her clothes and keeps moving. If she hurries, she has just enough time to swim before she has to pose again for her studio group in the afternoon.

It's a long day of work, both here and at home with the group, but she needs all the hours she can get. Lucy keeps telling her to come back to the Guild, save herself the trouble of arranging her own jobs. But Merav prefers the independence, not having to tolerate places and clients that she hasn't really chosen herself. And there were the times the Guild scheduled her in partnership with models that made her uncomfortable, strange men who might or might not know how to move alongside her in ways that felt right.

Lucy always says it's easy, like having safe sex from an even safer distance, or like dancing with a stranger.

Merav says, Not for me.

It wasn't just a question of contact or trust, but more that she wanted to be in that space by herself, wanted to feel her body's movements without having to pay attention to someone else.

Sex was different. Sex was all about that kind of shared attention. Joining one another in a zone deeper than breath, as if meeting underwater or in outer space. With so much skin so close to her own, with intimacy she had chosen, she could dissolve boundaries. Desire and its release could take her all the way out of her body.

But this wasn't sex. This was swimming in the air, alone.

Chapter Seven

IN THE FOURTH AND LAST HOUR, Danzig has backed away from his students completely, watching their absorption finally take hold. Only a handful are staying past the end of the class period, but this is the first time it's happened at all. Even if they don't realize it, he knows it must be because of M., because of the way she has given them permission to lose themselves, to get out of their own way.

A young man with curly black hair and a goatee and a nose ring is doing drawings in which M.'s body fills the page so completely she has become a series of abstract shapes, a landscape of shadow and light.

Yes, Danzig thinks. That one was really looking.

Dressed now, M. looks to him more ordinary, surprisingly so, and she still won't look directly into his eyes. She drinks from her thermos, leaning her head back, that pale skin exposed and calling to him. When he sees her getting ready to leave, he crosses the room quickly, almost colliding with her.

I have forgotten your name, he says, stepping backwards.

Merav, she says quietly.

What does it mean? he asks her. He is bracing himself now against the table where the stereo is set up. This Yo-Yo Ma recording is one of his favorite pieces, something he plays at home when he's trying not to think. He can see the movement of the music as it flickers in blue light just beside him on the digital readout.

It means more, she says.

More what?

Increasing something. Making it more than it is. Maximum.

Okay, he says, thinking, I'll call her M. anyway. It is of course an Israeli name, so she is Jewish, as he had guessed. No wonder she will not look him in the eye. He clenches his teeth.

Looking past her shoulder, he sees a wave of students leaving the room and notices that the waste bin near the door is filled to overflowing with abandoned pages. Danzig wants to teach them to claim their mistakes, so they can learn from them too. Sometimes he rescues the discarded drawings, uncurling them to talk to the class about what went wrong. But today he wants nothing more than to find a way to hold on to this woman.

I have a request, he says, almost blurting the words as she begins to turn away. I have a studio in Point Reyes. I'm always in need of a good model, and you're good. Would you work for me there?

She looks down at the floor, as if the answer might be found there. He accepts the hesitation, waits a few heartbeats.

I'd pay for your driving time, he says. That would be part of the deal.

Oh, she says.

There is a long, uncomfortable pause, which Danzig is tempted to fill with terrible thoughts. She doesn't trust him, doesn't want to have anything more to do with him; he will never see her again. He digs his hands into his pockets to keep from reaching out to touch her, knowing this could ruin all of it but almost desperate with the desire to keep her from leaving.

I'll have to think about it, she says, and then adds, Call the Guild. They'll know how to reach me. Her voice sounds strained, uncertain. For some reason he doesn't believe her.

But before he can say another word, she pulls her bag onto one shoulder and leaves the classroom, the door closing behind her with a little too much force. It is all he can do not to run after her or at least shout her name. But what is her name? It won't quite take rest in his brain, and he curses himself out loud.

The Guild, she said. He will have to ask them about her by describing her, by saying she's the Israeli one, or the one with the accent, though possibly there are several of those. He has never really wondered before.

She is, in any case, gone. For now.

He turns back to the classroom, expecting to find it empty, but seeing to his surprise that there are still three students remaining. One is working with her head down (the glaring girl! finally she is excited about something). Another two young men are talking with their hands, standing near his easel. When they see him looking in their direction, they practically bump into each other as they figure out how to approach him.

We want to ask you something, the taller one says. He wears a wool cap that mostly covers his dark hair; his wire-rimmed glasses are tipped unevenly on his nose.

The sketch on Danzig's easel is behind them. Danzig

wants to stand in front of it himself, study it for a moment alone, but here they are.

We never hear you talk about your own work, the tall one says.

The other one, a redhead with a beard and a prematurely receding hairline, shifts his weight from one foot to another as if he is getting ready to slouch off somewhere. He nods.

We can't help wondering, he says.

I'm Cliff, the redhead says, as if he sees suddenly in Danzig's face a lack of recognition.

And Jackson, says the other one.

Right, Danzig says.

The two of them turn toward the easel again. Cliff points. You hardly put anything there, he says. But there she is.

Jackson's turn to nod. It's wild, he says. I mean, I see it and I get it, but I don't get it. How a few lines can say all of this. He waves his hands, conjuring the ghost of her.

Danzig doesn't say anything. He looks at the drawing, sees M. with her back turning away from him, sees her spine curving like some ancient willow. She is already driving somewhere else by now, forgetting him completely.

So what about your paintings, says Jackson.

He is looking at Danzig now, blushing a little but at the same time openly curious, waiting. Of course they assume that he has work pouring out of him all the time, that it's out in the world, selling. That's what the school wants them to believe: if you get serious and focused and productive, your audience will find you. You'll be rewarded. That's one of his excuses for not ever talking about his own work, not wanting to encourage them, not wanting any of this to be about what's marketable, about the selling game. But who is he kidding.

Danzig sighs without meaning to. Then shrugs. There isn't anything right now, he says.

There's an uncomfortably long silence. Cliff is still studying the drawing.

Website? Jackson asks.

Danzig shakes his head. Not at the moment.

Cliff turns around, tugging at his beard and clearing his throat. What about more drawings, he says. I would love to see more like these. I mean, you know, to learn from them.

Danzig thinks about the man in New York City who for years made special requests to the gallery for his early drawings. For a long time, he too believed that his sketches were the most valuable work, though hardly anyone except that one buyer seemed to understand. Most collectors wanted the final results, while he was always most excited by the birth of the idea, the first vision. Torn slightly, bent at the corners, occasionally stamped with a footprint or splashed with coffee or wine, stained with real life. Imperfect and complete. Humble.

He steps past them and pulls the drawing off the easel, almost but not quite tearing it, wanting to show them it's nothing, and nothing matters.

See you next week, he says, dismissing them. The glaring girl has managed to leave without his noticing. Thank God for that, he thinks.

And suddenly, as if by a miracle, M. is there, in the doorway.

I forgot my thermos, she says. Fully three-dimensional,

not at all imaginary, she strides across the room to the chair where, sure enough, the thermos is leaning.

Cliff and Jackson say, in unison, Hey.

M. looks at the three of them, already halfway back toward the door.

You were great, Jackson says. Really great.

Thanks, M. says, over her shoulder.

Danzig doesn't even have a moment alone with her. Still, with adrenaline flooding him, he feels all his tiredness vanish, his disappointments wash away. Here it is: another chance to ask her to promise she'll work for him again, ask her name.

Something. Anything to keep her standing in front of him for more than a few seconds.

But he is too slow. The sketch is in his hand, but she is gone.

Chapter Eight

SHE HAD GOTTEN OUTSIDE the building and almost to the parking lot when she realized her bag wasn't quite heavy enough; something was missing from its weight. Hesitating, she spun on one heel and retraced her steps, resolute. The partial lie about the Guild echoed uneasily in her head, the reasons still unclear.

Students passing her in the opposite direction already looked unfamiliar, though she wasn't sure she would recognize any of them except maybe the one girl who reminded her of herself. There is often something awkward about seeing them afterwards, when she's been restored to her other, clothed self, when they are all a bit more equally hidden. Except, of course, they've seen her naked, so there is something else there, hovering.

The men usually appear the most uneasy, as if their desire has been exposed, or maybe their fear of it. She had made that one exception with Gabe, the client who became her lover and then her husband for a while. She had allowed herself that one extreme leap across the border, but she'd learned her lesson. More than ever, she knows what the limits are for.

LEAVING THE CLASS for the second time, anxious to be gone before Danzig tries to corner her again, Merav hears a conversation floating behind her in the hallway. Some of his students, the ones who were staring at his drawing of her, the ones who stayed late to talk to him. They must have left the room just after she did.

I knew it. I had a feeling.

Knew what?

That something was wrong.

All he said was, Not now. We were obviously in his face with asking. He wasn't in the mood. You know how he gets.

It's not just mood, I'm telling you. The guy is blocked, or something. He's teaching us, but he's not doing it.

Ask Valerie.

Who?

You know, the girl with the tongue stud. She can't stand him, thinks he's a fraud.

Merav stops listening. She has her own work to do, and the German man has already scratched her skin enough. She doesn't even have time to immerse in water before her group comes for the afternoon session in her studio.

LESS THAN AN HOUR LATER, Merav is setting up her studio for the Monday Group. She adjusts the room temperature, arranges the cushions, sighs with the relief of knowing that she is the only one who has been lying on them, her own bare feet the only ones on the pillows. Unlike the rest of her crowded appointments, here she can choose her own music, lighting, mood. This is a space of her own design, wearing the scent of her own body. An extension of her body.

The Monday Group came into being when Merav realized her schedule kept getting filled more and more quickly as her reputation grew. People started asking if they could book her on a weekly basis, if she could give discounts to starving artists, if they could work with partners. She discovered that by inviting a group to her own space she could charge them by the month, have a predictable cash flow, and give twelve artists a chance to work side by side.

She lives and works in a converted warehouse and garage in the Mission. It's the place she found after she and Gabe split up, the first place she's ever had that is her own. Every Monday afternoon, the same dozen artists arrange themselves in a semicircle of easels and chairs while she poses on a platform covered with her ever-changing assortment of cushions and tapestries and scarves.

One of the many reasons she loves Mondays is that she gets to pose surrounded by her own history, her sketches of the Sinai desert, the wall of open shelves on which she piles her clothes and books and blankets. The ceiling is stenciled with a net of tiny white Christmas lights. Several tables of various heights, scavenged from flea markets and garage sales, are covered with clusters of glue bottles, ink, feathers, postcards, unframed canvases, notebooks bulging with loose pages, art books, notepads. Maps, maps, maps.

These are the materials for her collages, the dreams she makes with her hands.

She loves maps not because she can read them but because they use a language she understands most fully in her imagination. The patches of green that speak of trees, flow-

ers, birdsong; the blue expanses or winding ribbons reminding her that land is only one third of the surface of the world,
subservient to water and pinned below an almost infinite
stretch of air. She traces highways with her fingertips, measures landscapes from thumb to pinky.

Periodically, Merav irons the maps, erasing their creases
except for a faint memory of white geometry; she wants
them to lie flat, flatter than the curve of the earth that holds
their dimensional counterparts. She spreads them on her
walls and tables, experimenting with their use as tablecloths,
wallpaper, lamp shades.

With a dozen people in her room, Merav feels her best.
With groups she can do poses that are a little too provocative
or too intimate for just one artist. In a room full of eyes she
can play freely with their voyeurism, wear her black strapped
heels and a black slip, turn her back and pose with the slip
pulled almost but not quite off, undressing as if in private for
an audience of ghosts.

She can sit on the edge of a chair and undo the strap of
one shoe, cross her body with a diagonal arm, a crossed knee.
Twist herself into a lyrical, seductive line. For all of them.

She is the answer and the question. The woman with the
body of a cello, the one whose curves they trace with their
pens and their brushstrokes. She wraps her arms around her
knees, turns her head, tilts her torso until it finds its shape in
the air. Conscious of every shadow, every angle and juxtapo-
sition, Merav knows how to make the design of her limbs
work from every seat in the studio, so that each of them finds
a place to focus on, a place from which to start.

This line here, this hollow, this parabola of throat or
shoulder or hip.

On her breaks, she wraps herself in a black silk kimono whose embroidered red dragon has eroded over the years, its scales disappearing like peeling skin. There is a large pot of coffee in the kitchen, a bowl of grapes or cookies. Someone always brings a loaf of bread or a bag of rolls, nuts, or crackers.

The artists don't talk much. They are here to work, not socialize. Sometimes during breaks Merav wanders among their easels, looking at the myriad versions of her body: the shadings at the small of her back and behind her knees, the way her fingers taper, the way her shoulder blades reflect light.

In the years that have passed since her first modeling session, she has often wondered what there is to recognize on their pages. She is smudged and abbreviated or elongated by a trick of the eye. Every once in a while, she senses a glimpse of the blue shadows hidden in her skin, the earthy color of her irises, the almost invisible scar beside the nipple of her left breast.

But of course there is so much they can't know about her, so much that is hidden even in the midst of so many hours and weeks of gazing.

Today, one of the women tells Merav they want to put together a show. Versions of Merav, she says they want to call it, or perhaps How We See Her. Merav reminds her that the point is to show their work, not focus on her, but Arlene says they know that.

It's just that you're what we have in common, Arlene says. You're at the center. Arlene is blushing.

Certainly, Merav feels they know more about her real life than the other artists she works for. They spend time in her studio, see her own drawings and designs, even see the insides of her kitchen cupboards and her bathroom shelves. They see the maps of the desert on her walls. In all these ways they can glimpse a bit of what she carries.

Each of the artists in the Monday Group has some idiosyncrasy that has become a kind of signature. Geoffrey always uses some sort of stick instead of a brush, scraping at his sketchpad with an ink-dipped branch. Linda usually spends the entire session on one vast and very populated page, allowing all of Merav's poses to overlap and collide. Sometimes she works on black paper with white crayons, inventing a crowd of ghosts. Arlene is the one who uses oversized books instead of sketchpads for her drawings. She finds old cookbooks, old dictionaries and atlases, and she paints on them. The one she gave to Merav now hangs on her wall. Her skin on the skin of the world.

The group packs up slowly, as if they're reluctant to leave. Arlene leaves last after standing for a while in front of Merav's bookshelves, studying her rows of Hebrew novels, English textbooks, art books. She carries a heavy canvas bag bulging with the spines of her painted-on volumes, the weight of it tipping her to one side.

Thank you, she says to Merav, the way she always does on her way out the door.

Alone again, finally giving way to her exhaustion, Merav turns off the music and runs herself a bath. She still feels the residue of her encounter with Danzig, the abrasion of his accent. So many old fears, the ones she still grapples with, even after her years in the army. The point of course had been to make her feel strong, fearless. She had felt that too, sometimes, felt the astonishing power of knowing how to shoot a gun, knowing how to kill.

She felt more competent even than she'd felt growing up on the kibbutz, where all of them believed they could do anything and everything. Physically and mentally they were prepared. The army was all about preparation too: about being alert to a hundred possible circumstances, having reactions fine-tuned and ready.

Her decision to live in the Mission had something to do with wanting to be surrounded by a blur of languages, a quilt of cultures and skin colors that reminded her of home. On her kibbutz, there were half a dozen families from Uruguay, and their melodious blend of Spanish and Hebrew had enchanted her.

In her teens, one of her Uruguayan friends had taught her some Spanish phrases, enough so that she now felt comfortable wandering into the Mexican shops and cafés surrounding her apartment building, greeting the owners. She listened to the rhythms pounding from car stereos, bought chilies and papayas to cook with, imagined that the heat of the Mexican deserts might feel something like the Sinai.

So many people in San Francisco came from somewhere else, suitcases filled with their own complex histories and desires. She kept collecting maps and wondered how long it would take her to become fluent in Spanish, whether she could ever truly decipher the tongues of her new neighbors. This meant not only knowing how to speak but how to understand, how to read the language of the body as well as the words spoken out loud. Her self-assigned mission was to blend in without forgetting who she was.

She recalls the intensive periods in the army when she spoke only Arabic, immersed herself in the sounds and metaphors of a culture that was part cousin and part alien to her own. She learned fast, using a talent she had been given. Her mother and grandmother between them had five languages, so Merav had an inherent facility, a good ear. The training was grueling and relentless, but of course her superiors in the army knew she had an aptitude for languages. She'd been tested on arrival, just like everyone else.

The painful part wasn't the overt training but the messages she began to feel seeping beneath her conscious awareness. She felt she was learning mistrust and hatred, even more than she'd been exposed to as a child growing up in a country surrounded by enemies. She was being trained to see others as killers who sought to annihilate her, her people, her way of life. She was learning to defend herself against an array of forces, learning to believe that saving her life could mean the taking of someone else's. And that was the equation she kept refusing.

THE BATH HAS CALMED HER, and she has allowed herself to forget about the day. But just as she's settling into bed with a cup of tea and a book of translated Norwegian poems, the phone rings. It's late and she won't answer it, but the machine picks up, and there it is: that German voice all over again.

I found you, he says. The Guild didn't know anything about you anymore, but Lucy was persuaded to give me your number. Don't be annoyed with her for doing it. I bullied her until she relented. I am a bully, but only for good reasons. So now I'm calling you, and I'm just going to do my best to ask you again nicely. Come and work for me. Please.

He leaves his phone number, and then there is a long silence, and then a dial tone. Merav holds her book and listens to herself breathing. The book is called *The Roads Have Come to an End Now,* and she can't remember why she owns it; someone must have given it to her. Or maybe she picked it up because of the title, the idea that every road has some sort of stopping place. In a way, her kibbutz was like that: a place where the road ended.

And now?

She will go to sleep. She will wait.

Chapter Nine

ON DANZIG'S DRIVE HOME, the sky is heavy and full of low-hanging clouds, blurred with fog and mist. This is the second of his two-days-a-week commute to San Francisco, and he's heading back to Point Reyes in the near dark, after the traffic has subsided. The driving is a misery sometimes, but there is no question that it's always worth it; each time he returns, he feels relief so palpable it seems to come from his bones.

For several years he kept a studio apartment in the city for weekdays, and it often proved convenient for the various trysts and seductions, a local bed within easy reach of the Institute. But now all he really wants is to get back to the country, back to the silence and open space it offers.

He's in the home stretch now, the part of the drive he loves best because everything about his students and the Institute and the city has receded. Usually he can tell himself that none of it exists. Like enormous pieces of his past, he can forget anything and everything, a series of doors closed and locked behind him.

Except tonight. He keeps hearing the sound of his own voice on what he hoped was M.'s answering machine, imagining it echo in her room, reaching out as if trying to press her against the wall, as if his mouth were close to her ear. For all he knows, she might simply erase the message without listening, wipe him off her skin like some kind of unwelcome dust. He will have to wait.

Meanwhile, there is his nightly visit to the studio. It's late enough not to bother at all. He could put it off until the morning, but with a very full glass of cabernet in his hand he goes into the barn and turns on a small lamp near the door. He notes the fog-dimmed moonlight pushing against the windows, inhales the cool moist air. Here are these familiar scents of turpentine and sawdust and paint, the blending of his sweat and sadness. He gulps at the wine, forgetting to taste it.

There are so many demons to face down tonight it hardly matters which one will show up first. They may have names or be among the nameless ones; maybe there are newcomers with the taunting voices of those students today, demanding proof that he has the right to teach them anything about anything.

The glaring girl, her pierced tongue pointing at him.

Jackson at his computer, searching in vain for Danzig's name.

His colleagues, avoiding him in the hallways, no longer even trying to get him to come to any of their meetings.

The secretaries in the office who barely meet his glance.

To hell with them.

Still standing close to the studio door, he is unwilling to enter any farther. The lamp throws a perfect circle onto the rough concrete floor, illuminating one vivid area stained with yellow paint from years ago. Above him the rafters are so high they have trapped the darkness overhead, and he doesn't even look up. Sometimes when he stands in here at night he can hear an owl calling into the sky from a nearby treetop. It's a sound that always makes him shiver, but tonight he can hear only himself.

The lamp he turned on is aiming its weak light toward the shadow-filled corner where an abandoned bathtub sits covered in old sheets. Nearby, filmed with dusty neglect, his canvases are stacked, turned away, all twenty-four of them. They are leaning, gleaming—all that whiteness in the dark, and the whiteness underneath the whiteness. Beckoning even with their backs turned and the bones of their wooden stretchers exposed. Prepared and expectant. Blank and terrifying.

To keep himself from painting the same paintings over and over, he had stepped all the way back from color and allowed himself only to prepare the base coats. Every morning he would place one prepared canvas on the easel and stare at it for hours; every night he would turn its face again to the studio wall. Something about avoiding the work kept it present in its possibilities.

All potential and no disappointment, no failure. The white silence allowing itself to be filled in the imagination, so that nothing had to be compromised or sacrificed. The ideal staying true to itself.

For a start he thought of it as a resting period, a time to find rejuvenation and inspiration, and really just to turn off the faucet. To stop. He would give himself six weeks without a paint-loaded brush in his hand—that was what he told himself. But it stretched into six months before he knew what was happening. Then longer.

When there were twenty-four of them, gesso-layered and long dried, he played tricks on himself. Cleaned brushes, organized piles of discarded sketches, rearranged supplies, destroyed old work he'd grown to hate. On and on. And on.

Sometimes, as if to convince himself there was a point to it all, he looked hard at the paintings he'd never finished but simply given up on, which in a way was how he felt about all of them, sometimes: that they were never finished but merely abandoned at the point where he felt finally that nothing more could be done with them.

It was what he admired about Bonnard, or at least what he loved about the famous stories in which Bonnard was applying paint to works already hanging in other people's houses. Something about never letting go, always feeling there was one more stroke to be added, one more note of the Unfinished Symphony. As if even death wouldn't be the ultimate form of completion but just another stop along the way.

HIS WINEGLASS IS EMPTY, and he is caught between going back inside for more wine or just standing here without its minor comforts for a little longer. He considers getting drunk and disconnecting the phone. But even in the midst of that thought he recognizes that he's been listening ever since he arrived for the sound of its ringing.

What comes to him are the names of the bones in the ankle, that taut band of the Achilles tendon, the valleys on either side. He convinces himself that he can even remember the details of M.'s body as distinct from that of any other model: the hollows inside her elbows, the vulnerable skin at the sides of her breasts, the blue veins of her wrists, the pink smudges at the edges of her eyelids.

He cannot explain it. Why desire comes to the surface in one place and not another, the mysteries of electric currents invisible yet so well delineated he could draw them. Between M. and himself, for example. A thick swath of red paint.

He can't yet say whether it is any different from how he'd first felt about Andrea. About Susan. He could count backwards through a string of others, but soon he'd get to the nameless ones. And somewhere back in the blur of his ancient history, there was even a distant cousin, some girl he probably saw once or twice at a contrived holiday gathering, introducing to him a mindless pulsing need that was never quite fulfilled.

And of course for occasional stretches of time there was nothing.

He used to think his heart had frozen, layers of ice and stone accumulating in the first years after leaving Germany, when all he knew how to feel was hatred and betrayal. The desperate need to place an ocean and then a continent between himself and his past, his father and the Fatherland. All behind him and of course (of course!) dragged like a tail that had been caught in a steel trap. No amount of gnawing at his own body could set him free. The metal banged and clattered at his heels like a relentless shadow.

WHAT IF HE HAS already done everything he could with what he was given; what if all of his stories and terrors don't have anywhere else to go? There could be a hundred more blank canvases ahead of him, white on white on white. A cemetery full of anonymous skeletons, decades of dust woven into his brushes. His studio full of dried paint and regret.

Meanwhile, Doctor Memento will dangle all summer in the classroom, waiting for Danzig to come back and say the same words all over again.

He hasn't made a new painting in five years.

Part Two

The Past

1982: Danzig

EACH TIME DANZIG WAS HANDED yet another glass of champagne, he imagined himself gulping it and smashing the crystal flute against one of the gallery walls. The impulse felt both exuberant and violent; he was vaguely aware of an inexplicable desire to destroy things as if to ward off disaster. But instead of disaster, Danzig was faced with actual and resounding success. It made him nervous enough to think that he might still turn around and hit someone, make one solid blow to a vulnerable jaw, breaking bones he could picture as in an X-ray. His hands practically twitched with an ache to make contact.

Somehow, though, he managed to drink in a more or less civilized manner and hand off the empty glasses to a waiter who seemed to be, at every perfectly timed moment, discreetly floating nearby. The bubbles eventually succeeded in calming his temper to the point where he wondered how soon he could get back home and into bed. He pictured himself climbing under the covers fully dressed, then waking the next day relieved beyond measure to see how empty his studio could be, its flat northern light bouncing against nothing.

CANDACE ATHERTON, the owner of her self-named gallery, though dressed entirely in white and apt to disappear in front of a white wall, kept orbiting into his peripheral vision. She seemed about to burst into flame, given how many red dots were already quietly and impressively littering the room.

Sold, sold, sold.

She had been right about everything, Danzig thought, including the guest list and the price list and even the flower arrangements.

Danzig watched the evening unfold as if it were a play, as if he were not a cast member or even a ticket holder in the audience but some object like the back wall of the theater, some immobile and invisible presence. He now leaned, in fact, against the gallery's only unadorned wall, the one nearest the door, which led to the elevator, which led outside, and therefore reassured him he could be the first escapee onto the street at any moment.

Thank God Candace was happy, he thought. And thank God even more that she already had a lover stashed away somewhere to help her celebrate later, so Danzig wouldn't have to figure out how to deliver those goods. She was a little too sexually hungry for his tastes; there was something more than vaguely predatory about her, something about the severity of her haircut and the sharpness of her high heels. He preferred doing the hunting himself, thank you. And in any case, he was far more interested in getting drunk tonight.

FROM WHERE HE STOOD, most of the paintings were obscured
by the crowd, and that was good too. Danzig had carefully su-
pervised their hanging, had made himself and everyone else
at the gallery crazy with his meticulous measuring and re-
measuring of the space, and it was beginning to occur to him
that at long last he wouldn't have to look at these paintings
anymore. They would hang in other people's houses, gathering praise or indifference without his knowledge.

He had worked on this series for nearly six years. Whatever had been haunting him, whatever had poured out of
him in a fever of despair or rage—all of that was done now,
dried and complete.

Maybe now the images would finally leave him alone.

These twenty pieces were all officially untitled, identified
only by number and an occasional reference to color. Untitled in Gray #3, or simply Untitled #11. But for Danzig, in
his mind's private gallery, each painting was invisibly en-
graved with a phrase held like a repeating song fragment,
even though he had no idea where the words came from.
Some might have been poetry he had read, or bits of overheard conversations in cafés and bars. Some might have origi-
nated in daydreams. Or nightmares. There was "we are still
alive amid so many dead people." There was "let the sky between you and me be cut into shreds." There was "the fragrance of eyelashes." There was "the possible is not enough."
There was "in what language?"

For six years he had worked on these wall-sized canvases,
their dimensions dwarfing him by day and by night. Sometimes he had to use a stepladder just to reach the edges of

the work. Subject to moods as changeable as the weather, he hurled paint from a distance and scraped at it up close. The walls of his rented studio on Army Street suffered blows of disappointing cobalt or furious vermillion. Each of the windows above his head was covered with translucent white paper bearing splattered stains that might have been some giant's Rorschach tests. The couch and all four mismatched chairs looked as though they too had been used for palettes. Nothing was spared when his brush was in motion.

Danzig was the only one who knew just how many layers these paintings held prisoner, the secrets hidden under their skin.

What lasted in the end were the imaginary ghost towns of those exposed apartments he had memorized so long ago, populated with dozens of figures painted out but still vaguely visible as pentimenti under semi-opaque white. Hanging nearby, too, were empty streets with snowy footprints and an abandoned bicycle. Figures were implied in the shadows of every cityscape, even present—as if glimpsed out of the corner of one's eye—in the forest, but never distinct.

And resonating like a bass note throughout: the color of hopeless mornings.

He knew what he had painted. And he knew what he had not yet been able to touch.

THIS WAS HIS YEAR, his month, his moment. He had shown his work before, in smaller group shows and as part of his degree program a decade earlier. But this was like launching into space, and his prices were suitably astronomical.

Leaning against all of the walls in his studio, Danzig's

paintings had murmured or groaned in the private voices of his past. But here in the Atherton Gallery, in their temporary new habitat, they began to announce themselves not only as dreams in a foreign language but as expensive objects of desire.

Candace whispered to him that her favorite reviewer from the *San Francisco Chronicle* was delirious with excitement. Danzig would be both rich and respected, mastering the ever-elusive dance of fortune and talent.

A waiter brought him another glass of champagne.

Meanwhile, the board of the Art Institute, having hired Danzig one semester at a time as they watched for his star to rise or fall, had waited to see whether his reputation would do them any good. Now he was leaping into the firmament. No doubt this would turn them toward wondering whether he might quit teaching in the name of his own success.

Later that night, or maybe in another week, he would draft a letter of resignation. He was through with the classroom, he said to himself, almost muttering the words aloud. How much more could he give away to his students? How many more days and weeks could he afford to lose in the name of someone else's need for inspiration? The Institute had been a good safety net for a while, and he had made a kind of home there. But now it was time to turn toward the unknown. He could take new chances.

As for the immediate future, his plans were simple: he had a late-morning appointment the very next day with a Realtor to look at property in the verdant county of West Marin. Something close to the wild open sea, instead of held near the tame enclosure of the bay. The idea was to live just far enough away from San Francisco to make him feel like a landowner but close enough to the city to keep his stimulants accessible. On the phone, he told the Realtor what he envisioned: a small house and a large barn and neighbors he could ignore with impunity.

Point Reyes had been one of his first discoveries after arriving in California, and every time he drove onto that vast peninsula, hiking out to watch the elk in mating season or to stare for hours at the fierce surf, he felt himself breathing freedom. For years, he had fantasized about what it would be like to live there, what it would be like to visit the urban grid and leave it behind when he had had enough.

No, I won't be commuting, he told the Realtor when she asked.

This would be his reward for persevering against all odds, for banking on the power of his imagination and desire, for knowing how to turn pigment into visible music.

Candace had already written him a check for the seven paintings sold before the show had opened, buyers who considered themselves lucky to have an inside track to her latest discovery. At least two of them, Candace explained, were considered to be among the most foresighted collectors in the country.

You'll see, she said. People will be clamoring for more of you.

Danzig deposited the money into his bank account immediately, struck by the astonishing idea that he could suddenly buy whatever he wanted, even a house in the country. And there would be enough money to keep his studio in San Francisco too.

This was exactly the kind of feeling that most people

would use in making a triumphant return home, he thought. All the way back to the origins of their earliest dreams.

His mentor Hoffman was the only one he could imagine shouting the news to, the only one who might have truly been proud. He used to imagine that Professor Hoffman might even be impressed to know that Danzig was teaching, following that path too.

All those steady years of working alone, feverish with memories that he had to expel, and Hoffman's stern patience, his predictions about Danzig's future as a painter.

It's happened, he wanted to say. I've made it.

But Hoffman was dead. Danzig's childhood friend Mateus, in his last of several unanswered letters, had sent to Danzig in California the small clipping of Hoffman's obituary.

Thought you would want to know about this, Mateus had scrawled. And then, with more sarcasm: Since I gather from your silences that you want to be left alone, I won't write again. Good luck with your life.

Danzig was thirty-six years old. There was no one left who mattered.

1991: Danzig

TYPICALLY FOR A TUESDAY MORNING, Danzig fortified himself
with a full breakfast at the Pine Cone Diner before heading
south toward San Francisco, bracing himself for the hour of
freeway chaos en route to the Institute. His car waited out
front, parked with its nose facing a group of picnic tables.
The wind was pulling in the right direction, which meant his
breakfast wasn't accompanied by the perfume of manure
from the nearby ranch.

The predictably surly waitress who didn't speak to him always got a generous tip for leaving him alone. For entertainment, he read the local weekly paper, the *Point Reyes Light*,
especially the section "Sheriff's Calls": a laundry list of
break-ins and near-disasters that always made him laugh.
Reports of allergy attacks and obscene phone calls and people who "acted as if they wanted to fight" took their usual
place alongside concerns about wounded raccoons, the smell
of propane, and cars scratched in the night.

Danzig ordered his green chile omelet and drank too
much coffee, keeping resentful track of time.

In one of the other booths in the diner, Danzig recognized
an acquaintance who had begun to advertise classes in *plein
air* painting, dragging around kids and retired people who
wanted to try standing at easels and making a mess for a few

hours at a time. He found himself nearly furious at the idea, almost as disgusted by this as he was bothered by the aging hippies on their motorcycles who parked outside the Bovine Bakery, comparing muscles and toys. He watched them with contempt and ridicule even as he understood that he might one day appear something like them—perhaps, he hoped, with a bit more privacy for his wreckage.

At some undetermined moment during the past nine years, he had managed to become a local, routinely using his own mug at the bakery and being referred to by name at the post office. Somehow everyone seemed to know he was a painter, though he never participated in the annual open studios, and his work was never seen in town. He was perhaps most famous for keeping to himself. His phone number was unlisted.

Outside the diner, turkey vultures perched on a utility wire, taking turns at some unfortunate dead thing in the road. A deer, maybe. Just the other day he'd seen a red-tailed hawk with a mouse in its talons, and though he didn't believe in omens, it made him shiver anyway. Raptors are raptors, he thought. Hunting and killing: it's what they do. The mouse looked alive and in shock, or so Danzig imagined, though he tried not to think too much beyond what he had already witnessed. The doomed prey was off the ground by about thirty feet, and the thought of being grabbed and hoisted like that made him dizzy.

That was yesterday. Today, he had a class to teach.

HIS SECOND MEAL OF THE DAY, after his class ended, took place in another restaurant, this time just a few blocks from the

Art Institute. He had long since given up on the school cafeteria, plagued by its familiarity and cacophony. It was no good trying to be mean and aloof, grimacing and silent: his students kept approaching him in the middle of a sandwich or with coffee not quite bitter enough to cure a hangover. Finally he understood they would never leave him alone as long as he remained within reach.

Just that morning he had decided to spend the next six weeks drawing with his left hand, making everything a little uncomfortable and a little out of control. It was a trick, but he was greatly in need of one. He sat looking out at the street traffic and tried to ignore the painfully nasal whine of the customer near his table. Now would be a good time for some beauty, he thought.

And as if he had conjured her, a new waitress appeared in a midriff-baring T-shirt with her name on a plastic tag pinned above her right breast. Andrea. She looked to him like the Goddess of America, freckled and wavy-haired and golden-skinned, full of natural light like the light he saw everywhere in the landscapes around Point Reyes. She looked better than a good slice of pie. A safe haven, a twenty-something woman with a simple willingness to bring his food and smile without any apparent effort.

Once Danzig began to keep track, though, he noticed that he was receiving just about the same frequency and quality of smiling that all the other male customers received. Without taking himself too seriously, he scribbled a note on the back of his lunch bill, asking if she had any interest in posing for him sometime.

I teach up the street at the Institute, he wrote.

She read the note with her back turned, so he couldn't tell

whether she was blushing or annoyed or having any other of a hundred possible reactions.

Attempting and failing to read her body language, he placed three extra singles on the table. What the hell, he thought. It's just one of those days.

But Andrea astonished him by coming back over to his table and asking him to tell her more.

Danzig smiled. He told her that she was softer than a lot of the women he usually noticed. She appeared a bit puzzled, possibly offended.

Is that supposed to be a compliment? she asked.

You know what I mean, he said, and went on to over-explain that she was graced with long limbs that apparently didn't require the kind of muscular elaboration that seemed so ubiquitous.

Well, I happen to like looking feminine, she said.

And this pleased him as a rare and almost original thought, considering the variety of gender disguises he had become accustomed to at the Institute.

He told her he wanted to use her as a model for a painting he was working on that might or might not actually include figures by the time it was finished. Even to himself it sounded both weak and pretentious, a tedious come-on, but she astonished him by saying Yes.

One condition, she added. I have to bring along my body-guard.

Her blue eyes twinkled like something out of a second-rate movie, and Danzig was about to turn the whole thing into a joke. But then she pointed to a sleeping mound of fudge-colored fur under one of the corner tables.

He's a good dog, she said.

ANDREA'S PRESENCE in Danzig's Army Street studio seemed temporarily to bring the place some additional quality of brightness. Bruno, dragging his leash, circled the room, sniffed at all the furniture, and curled with what looked like resignation into one dusty corner. Andrea filled a dish with water at the sink and placed it near Bruno's noble profile.

Sweet dreams, she said.

Danzig tried not to focus on the way the air tended to feel a bit trapped, and the fact that the fridge contained two bottles of chardonnay and nothing else but forgotten lemons dried into stone. Now that she was here, all of his attention turned toward making sure she stayed within reach. The major problem showed up only for him, in the form of echoing reminders of his old work. The walls still held the splattered remains of his big paintings, left over from the ones Candace Atherton had sold so quickly and lucratively. Untitled Series of Twenty. 1982.

Don't ask about it, he said, attempting a breezy tone and waving dismissively at the blank rectangles on the walls.

Andrea seemed perfectly calm so far. He decided she was either concealing her nervousness with great skill or possibly feeling she had the upper hand. Danzig poured them each a glass of wine and set up a sheet-draped chair with a good view of the dog. Are you okay with this? he asked.

She raised an eyebrow. Getting undressed in front of a strange man, you mean?

You can start with clothes on, if you prefer, he said.

She actually closed her eyes to think it over. I suppose so, she said.

Danzig adjusted the angle of the chair, momentarily regretting the entire event. Bruno thumped his tail against the floor, chasing something in his sleep.

Andrea laughed. I can do this, she said. Really.

For the first half hour she was a mock ballerina, a cover girl, an exotic dancer. She tried on expressions and discarded them, finally asking Danzig what he wanted her to do.

Be yourself, he said. Relax.

In honor of her bravery, Danzig experimented with an ochre-loaded brush, skipping the drawing stage altogether and moving directly to paint. When she began to take shape in elongated, hazy curves, it seemed as if Danzig's favorite Marin landscape had merged with her body. If she had been in the other studio, in Point Reyes, it might have seemed redundant. But with the roar of Army Street traffic outside, she became a reminder of his other life, a souvenir of nature.

Her body revealed itself exactly the way he had imagined it under her waitress outfit, although there were surprises he couldn't have predicted. Pale pink nipples, for example, and tan lines from a very small bikini. He had already noted her very long leg muscles, but now they were available for closer inspection.

Long walks with Bruno, she said.

The fine gold hair on her forearms and thighs, almost the surface of an apricot, made him desperate to touch her.

No biting, he said to himself. Not yet.

But the resolve lasted for only an hour, perhaps two. At his insistence, they each had a second glass of wine, and though Andrea demurely wrapped herself in a sarong during a break, Danzig peeled it off without hearing a single note of objection. She tasted like ripe fruit. Firm and fragrant and juicy.

The sheets on his bed were musty, but he didn't care. Sweet Andrea actually purred with pleasure, making him feel heroic and unusually generous. She stretched her voluptuous legs and waved her arms like a dancer on vacation, her skin catching the early evening light. They might have drifted off to sleep together, until Danzig suddenly noticed the paint under his fingernails, caught a whiff of turpentine on his own skin.

And that was when the devastating truth arrived, breaking over his head like a terrible wave.

Now it was too late to go back and reclaim his position on the other side of the easel, too late to re-create some essential space between them. He had squandered the electricity that might have brought the work to life. It poured out of his body and into hers, absorbed and lost.

"We worked no more that day," Modigliani once wrote, after one of his models proved irresistible and her distractions forced the brushes out of his hands.

AT THEIR SECOND MEETING and then the third, Danzig only confirmed what he already knew. Silent and miserable, even as he lay pasted to her body with his drying sweat, Danzig felt a fool, disappointed not in her but in himself because he should have known better. After all these years of finding and discarding models, he'd made the mistake all the same. Such an old story. She goes from Muse to Lover, and all the magic vanishes, all the fascination and mystery kept alive by way of distance, all of it dissolved and ruined when he gets too close.

Even with the series of meetings, they seemed to exchange hardly more than a few sentences. Danzig was grateful to have had the foresight to pay her in advance the final time, relieved that the awkward departure would be spared that element, at least. Andrea almost left a pair of silver earrings behind, glinting beside the kitchen sink with what felt to Danzig like some sort of regret.

Let's see what happens next, she said mysteriously.

Danzig said, I'll call you.

Each time, Bruno seemed increasingly delighted to be leaving.

IN A CONTINUATION of his own version of the story, he convinced himself that Andrea was the one who was disappointed. He forced himself to stay away from her restaurant for several weeks, ashamed of his own cowardice but unwilling to overcome it. Finally, he forced himself to go in for lunch more than a month after their third encounter, bracing himself for some false cheerfulness, or possibly disdain. Instead, she gave him a dark look and said, Let's talk out back.

Unwinding the apron from around her hips and leading him by the hand, she pulled him through the narrow, steam-filled kitchen to the shade-dimmed patio. Through an open door, the dishwashers chattered in Spanish amid the sounds of machinery and sloshing water. Danzig stood with his hands in his pockets, watching Andrea's face with a growing sense of dread.

I'm pregnant, she said.

He stopped himself from asking if the child was his. And

anyway, Danzig thought she was on the pill; wasn't that what she told him? And of course she was going to have an abortion?

I'm thirty-three, she said, and she placed her long-fingered hands on her still perfectly flat belly.

This information surprised him somehow, though he realized he had never even bothered asking her age. Then again, they hadn't really talked about anything. Where was she from? He had no idea.

The patio behind the restaurant reeked of rotting vegetables, and Danzig felt caught in some terrible film where his own script had somehow been lost.

She could model for him during her pregnancy, she said. She could wait and see if he might fall in love with her.

Danzig kept his eyes on the cement beneath his feet, hating how the weeds pushed up through the cracks. He thought of that first day with her in the studio, the looks that had passed between them until they finally tore at each other in his bed. That gleam of desire, he now reflected—maybe that was a fever for trapping him, possessing something he had never meant to offer.

Andrea continued talking about the baby, about her family in Iowa where she grew up, about how much she had always wanted a child.

What could he possibly say to remain unaccountable? It was hard enough taking care of himself, he said at last, bypassing her face and staring straight up at the sky. He never wanted to be anyone's father.

From there, the conversation stopped. If she had pleaded, it might have been even worse, but they both went cold at once. Someone called "Order's up, Andrea" from inside the kitchen, and she looked at Danzig with an expression of utter contempt.

I understand, she said. I'm on my own.

THE LAST THING HE HEARD from her was by way of a hand-written letter mailed to him at the Institute. Before opening it, Danzig studied the postmark from Iowa, and for a few minutes, he worked at mentally sketching a happy outcome. He pictured Andrea with her full-moon belly in a flat land-scape in the middle of the country, a place he had never seen or tried to imagine in any detail. She would have stayed beautiful out of spite, he thought, and then he conjured for her some farmer husband who would make a place for her in his life, cornfields all around.

Instead, her scrawled curses scarred him like the after-math of an animal attack: Danzig would never get to meet his son, even if he changed his mind in twenty years. She would tell the child his father was dead. And she wished for Danzig a long and tormented life in which one woman after another would devote herself to making his life insufferable. Especially, she hoped, ruining his art forever.

EXACTLY SIX WEEKS LATER, providing another remedy that would prove worse than the disease, Susan arrived. A visiting artist who had been invited to teach an intensive course on printmaking at the Institute, she caught his body's attention immediately, although he assumed she was a new student, maybe in the graduate program.

More dangerous than that, said one of Danzig's col-

leagues, after both of them watched Susan climb the stair-
case ahead of them, splendid in ripped jeans and a black
sweater. According to Wallace, who knew everything about
everyone, she was visiting for half the semester. This information quietly and significantly registered in Danzig's awareness as a perfect safety valve. Temporary insanity seemed
exactly what he needed.

He had reluctantly been returning to the school cafeteria,
Andrea's restaurant having left much too bitter an aftertaste.
The Institute had a balcony with one of the best panoramic
views in the city, taking in Alcatraz and the Golden Gate,
great expanses of Marin and the East Bay hills too. Danzig
had to admit that this vista was occasionally worth suffering
through unsought conversations with students. On a perfectly blue afternoon, Susan sat alone in a pair of movie-star
sunglasses, looking out at the spectacular scenery. Danzig
brought his coffee and sat beside her on a bench, pretending
she needed protection from hormone-charged artists.

Bizarre idea, she said, laughing, and then turned toward
him, taking off her dark shades to reveal a pair of green,
mock-serious eyes. You know a little too much about the student body yourself, I'd say.

He refused to laugh but stayed on the bench anyway,
noticing that this woman seemed to have several faces, profiles he didn't quite like. It was her head-on asymmetry that
worked best, he decided, a frank gaze aimed directly at him.

With minimal discretion, he examined her from up close:
her too-large breasts in contrast to her narrow waist and slender limbs, the blackness of her hair against her very pale
skin. Something about her nervous gestures and gnawed fin-

gernails set off warning bells, but he ignored them, fascinated by an irresistible heat.

They talked about the Institute, its quirky underpaid staff. She told him that Wallace had made a pass at her on the first day of class.

And? Danzig asked.

I'll tell you a story if you tell me one first, she said.

Without meaning to take her up on the offer, he found himself telling her about Andrea. It was so recent, still infuriatingly sharp. He heard himself sounding like the victim, not entirely innocent but at least not deserving of so much venom at the end.

So you feel duped? she asked. Taken for a ride?

She was just an Iowa farm girl trying to get happy, he said. And apparently I fucked things up. He laughed with a kind of relief, realizing that in the end, he didn't actually care. Susan kept turning her various profiles on him, surveying the view, not saying anything for a while.

It's your turn, he said. Tell a story.

She replaced her glasses, concealing that green spark. Over dinner, she said.

Somehow, without his guiding them there, Susan seemed to be making it abundantly clear that she was just waiting for the right invitation. She leaned into him on the way to his car, offering her body as if Danzig was entitled to the consolation. And he never once considered refusing the gift until it was too late.

As a houseguest staying with friends she had no bed to invite him into, so he brought her to Army Street, buying them burritos and beer at his favorite local dive on the way.

What a fancy seduction, Susan said, but then insisted on taking a long walk through the Mission before agreeing to come all the way home with him. I've got a reputation to maintain, she said. No sex with the senior faculty.

The word Senior hit hard, and he said as much. I've been meaning to retire for the past decade, he said.

Susan laughed again and shadowboxed with him for good measure. Get a sense of humor, she said.

DANZIG'S NEAR-OBSESSION with Susan's angular beauty began to haunt him as soon as he saw her writhing against his white sheets. Something about the way she inhabited herself in so many directions made him think at first that he needed not only a new palette but possibly a new form altogether, a field with more dimensions. It occurred to him that maybe in sculpture there would be less torment than the way he felt grappling with a painting that seemed to want to kill him.

For almost a month, he and Susan met several afternoons a week in his Army Street studio: every one of the days he taught, and even one extra that he would ordinarily have used for staying in Point Reyes. He amazed himself with the degree of desire he felt, electric and unmanageable.

For her part, she seemed particularly to enjoy prolonging the moments before he was allowed to touch her, teasing him from across the room and sometimes threatening to leave without any sex at all, just to make sure his desire was never quite satisfied.

I've got my own work to do too, you know, she said. And here I am giving away all the inspiration to you.

Danzig heard this both as an accusation and some claim

of her own power; possibly both were true. He found himself using his hands in new ways, experimenting with clay and stone and wood, trying to find a medium that might hold her or keep her from escaping his grasp. He watched the movement of light on the planes of her face, those seemingly infinite angles of expression and mystery. Sometimes he thought she wasn't beautiful at all, just a constantly changing layer of skin across bone, a river of mood that never stood still.

She watched his fingers massage her calves, watched them move back and forth between her clay body and the real one. She said she was the one reinventing him, believed it was the elixir of her passion transforming him.

Wallace, naturally, guessed what was going on and attempted to find out more from Danzig. Wasn't I right? he said. About the dangerous thing . . . ?

They were out on Chestnut Street at the end of the day, leaving for their respective other lives. Danzig knew from Susan that nothing had happened with Wallace, and he was sure as hell not going to give him anything juicy of his own. This was the kind of thing men liked to do— compare notes about women—but somehow he was certain this would be for Wallace almost as good as having sex with Susan himself.

Danzig shook his head, refused to offer any confidences. Private matters, he said.

Later that afternoon, Susan began to make noises about staying on longer, seeing whether she could find a more permanent teaching position somewhere.

I'm really happy here, she said. And this neighborhood is so great.

They were walking back toward his studio from a café on Valencia Street. Danzig suddenly felt that all he wanted for the night was to sleep, alone, and yet here he was. Here *she* was.

I've been spending too much time in the city, he said, thinking how much he was missing his silence, his distant, greener world.

I could come out there to Point Reyes with you, she said. Maybe set up a work space for myself too.

The semester was going to be ending soon, and Danzig knew perfectly well that the last thing he wanted was long-term company. The summer was his best chance for new work, his wide-open landscape of no commitments. He had lately begun considering some projects with metal, sharp edges and tools, torches and high temperatures. Melting and pounding, making hard things yield.

Susan was supposed to be long gone by then.

What about Chicago? he said. I thought you had things to do back there.

She stopped on the sidewalk and turned toward him, pulling his hands into her hair. I'm not so sure, she said.

He untangled his hands and started walking again. Summers are cold here, he said.

Hey, she said, jabbing him in the ribs. Nobody said it's all about you. Calm down.

Back in the studio, Susan sat on the edge of his bed and Danzig paced nearby, not quite knowing how to conceal his annoyance. She was taking up too much room, pulling relentlessly at his attention. He poured them each a glass of wine, and she turned a questioning eye toward him, yanking off her shoes and kicking them into a corner.

I'm tired, he said.

She snorted, hit a pillow with the back of her hand. You mean you're tired of me, she said.

Danzig remained silent, making a move for a chair on the far side of the room.

I see you watching those slutty students of yours, she added. She gulped at her wine and then suddenly jumped up to reach for Danzig's glass, putting both glasses down with a bit too much force on the table near the bed. Her next move was to start tearing off her clothes, throwing things.

Listen, he said, deliberately keeping his voice low. Maybe this isn't a good night for anything but sleep.

She said Ha with a sharp burst of breath and continued undressing, snatching the covers off the bed and hurling pillows against the nearest wall. Let's fight, she said. Come on.

Danzig stood up and heaved a sigh, realizing this was a good time to move the glasses of wine out of the way. Cabernet was about to go flying, he guessed.

I'm tired, he said again. Just that.

I don't care, she said, and then she dropped to the floor, grabbing at Danzig's legs, trying to lift up one of his feet and practically throwing him off balance. Take off your shoes, she said, her voice husky. Take off everything.

His laugh came out almost like a grunt. No, he said.

I'm serious, she said. Please.

He backed out of range, taking the wineglasses with him. But Susan wouldn't stop. She crawled forward and leaned hard against his legs, then began pulling him back toward the bed, swiping at his arms and hands. The glasses went airborne, splashing wine and shattering crystal.

For a moment, Susan's eyes went wide, then she scrambled back onto the bed. Perfect, she shouted.

Danzig stared at her, the pale accusation of her skin against his sheets. He turned a slow circle and regarded the broken glass, the stains at his feet. Good thing his shoes were still on, he thought.

Susan held her arms open, beckoning. She said, Forget that stuff.

Danzig laughed with derision this time, feeling his bitterness rising. Game over, he said.

He bent down to retrieve some of Susan's clothes, tossing them at her one at a time. When he shook out her shirt, hearing some glass loosened from its folds, he found himself thinking that maybe it would do her some good to get cut, just a little. The idea made him flinch, but there it was: he wanted to see her bleed.

We are done here, he said, slowly, emphatically. But Susan sat unmoving on the bed, allowing the clothes to land all around her. She glared and curled a lip at him.

I'm not done, she said.

Danzig crossed toward the bed, hearing the glass crunch underfoot. He would throw her naked out the door if that was what she wanted.

Time to go, he said. Reaching for her shoulders, he prepared to lift her off the bed, just as she slid away and aimed downward, aiming for the shards of glass. Before he could prevent it, she rolled onto the floor, gathering pinpoints of glass that quickly turned her back into a constellation of bloody stars. He grabbed her by the hair, yanking her to her feet, even as she tried to pull handfuls of broken glass with her.

They were both snarling now, practically spitting at each other. Susan kicked as he carried her by her armpits into the bathroom, her back bleeding in small rivulets, smearing his hands. When he let her feet touch down, she buckled at the knees, clawing at him like some feral thing. He felt his heart pounding, his pulse wild at his temples. And that was when he hit her, catching her fully on the cheek, staining her in the shape of his palm.

I hate you, she screamed. You bastard, I hate you.

Danzig slammed the bathroom door behind him as he left, trapping her inside. The echo of his parents' voices seemed to crash like surf in his head, the unforgettable sounds that used to come from their bedroom. Mutti's bruised face in the morning, half-hidden under her loose hair. Papa's big hands, slamming onto Danzig's back and legs.

He stood with his fists clenched and realized he was panting. Then he walked toward the bed, consciously trying to steady his breath. Gathering up Susan's clothes and shoes, he went to reopen the bathroom door and found her staring hard at her own reflection, a towel on her shoulders. There was no blood seeping through it, so that meant the cuts weren't deep.

Get out, he said, thrusting her clothing into her hands, forcing his voice to stay low and steady. Get out now.

She threw the towel on the floor and started putting her clothes on, tossing her hair, swearing under her breath. When the apartment door banged shut behind her, all he could think to do at first was throw the dead bolt and hit the wall with both hands, palms wide.

There were bloody footprints on the bathroom floor, shattered glass to sweep away. The spilled wine had already begun to dry in streaks around the room. Let it all stay here, he thought. And then, following blind urges around the studio, he began laying hands on the half-finished work he had tried to make of her, the distorted pieces of clay and stone and wood. Cracking and splintering and crushing them into dust.

If he had been in Point Reyes, he would have started a bonfire, burning things into oblivion.

He was not a monster. She couldn't do that to him. He could erase her.

BUT SOMETHING IRREPARABLE had broken inside him. Danzig woke up late in the dismal morning, canceled class to return to Point Reyes. Even there he couldn't find a way to restore himself. He considered avoiding the Institute entirely until he was certain Susan was gone, but somehow he managed to focus the remnants of his energy on student evaluations and the end of classes. He heard that Susan had vanished from the school without another word.

Wallace watched him in the hallways, looking for clues. After a while, Danzig actually mouthed at him Fuck off when he saw Wallace coming down the hall.

Day after day, week after week, he had nothing to say to anyone, and the summer fog rolled in like a numbing blanket, matching his gray mood. His hands and his heart were silent. He felt like an ancient painting with fugitive colors, the pigments that decompose and vanish. Prolonged exposure to air and light and time itself made them disappear.

At night in his living room, he drank vengeful toasts to the collector in New York who had bought so many of his drawings, including a recent series of Andrea and then Susan. There was nothing he could do about his aching need to destroy those too. He had to live with them out in the world, no longer his to frame or incinerate.

The Atherton Gallery suggested taking a break for a while, concerned, Candace said, about Danzig's unpredictable output. He had promised her a first look at the new sculpture, and now he had to tell her to wait. Possibly forever. Of course the devoted collector seemed to disappear then, too, having lost interest or simply moved on to someone else, to the next astonishing talent. Candace of course would have wanted that: to redirect a buyer's greedy gaze and therefore his checking account.

On top of everything else, the idea that he had a son somewhere, who could be anywhere, and without any ideas about his father except whatever lies Andrea might provide— that idea made him weep with even more humiliated rage. It was a nightmarish variation on the theme of his own exile, his refusal to stay in contact with his parents. They were all dead by now, without his knowing when or how.

Just when he thought he was backed into the final corner of his life, hopelessly paralyzed, a phone message came from Wallace with news that sent Danzig into a state of total blackout.

Susan attempted suicide in Chicago, Wallace's voice said. Nobody knows why.

After a long pause, he continued. She's okay now, I guess. He cleared his throat. I thought you might want to be informed.

Wallace's voice went quiet and then resumed.

The Institute got the word from some relative who was

looking to see whether there might have been any indica-
tions of instability, that kind of thing. It turns out she'd tried
it twice before. Pills, I think. Something like that. I'm ram-
bling now. But that's the story. I hope your work is going well,
somehow or other. I'll see you in the fall.

Danzig was standing in the kitchen when he heard the
message, holding a knife and a loaf of fresh sourdough bread.
It was the first solid food he had attempted all day, and now
he looked at it as though it were made of sawdust.

No, he said out loud. Not this.

1964: Danzig

THE BRUSHES were missing.

Danzig should already have been on his way to Herr Hoffman's class, but he couldn't find his favorite paintbrushes, and he couldn't leave without them. He had been hiding his art supplies at his friend's house, but the situation had changed. Mateus said his father was rummaging in his room and almost threw the brushes away, thinking they must have belonged to a former tenant. Wrapped in rags, the brushes could have been mistaken for garbage, it was true, but Danzig groaned when Mateus told him what had almost happened.

Never mind, he said. I'll keep them in my room somehow.

But for a moment he couldn't remember where he'd placed them, and in a rising panic, he began lifting his mattress, crawling under the bed frame, and diving into the back of his closet. His heart banged in his chest like something trying to get out of a locked room.

There.

Inside a pair of old boots and safe.

He stuffed the bundle into his knapsack and headed downstairs, grabbing what was left of a loaf of bread and some cheese to eat on the way. Calling out his good-byes, he pulled the door closed behind him and took a deep breath to calm his still-pounding heart. No one tried to stop him this time, and he had gotten away with time to spare.

It was three weeks after Danzig's eighteenth birthday, and he had been conducting a secret life as an art student for several years. He told his parents elaborate lies about friends, about membership in a hiking club, playing on a soccer team, although in truth it seemed they were not paying much attention. He made up anything that seemed likely to explain the amount of time he spent out of the suffocating house, leaving behind the kitchen walls scarred from too many hurled dishes, the whiskey-stained carpets and patched curtains. Every battered object told yet another story.

Often when Danzig walked or bicycled past the reconstructed apartment building whose solid brick walls now concealed all of its inner life, he found himself thinking about his sister, Margot. Despite the hundreds of times he had revisited their last conversation on the upturned vegetable crate, he had never quite arrived at an explanation for what happened. The question haunted him like the sound of far-off train whistles in the dark. And neither of his parents ever mentioned her name.

Meanwhile, his daydreams carried him farther from home and deeper into the landscape of imagination. His art teacher, Herr Hoffman, though he was often gloomy and sharply critical of Danzig's work, seemed to take a particular interest in him, even giving him a key to the art studio and gruffly assuring Danzig that he was allowed to come early and stay late.

If you care enough to devote yourself, go ahead, Hoffman said. Passion doesn't come around in every lifetime, you know, so make the most of it.

Although Danzig never explained why, Hoffman appeared to understand that he needed a sanctuary. Even with the assignments given by Hoffman to copy old masters and practice purely technical drawing, Danzig found pleasure and liberation. When his eyes and hands felt engaged this way, he could freely ignore the rest of the world; the spinning of his mind stopped, and time no longer mattered. Sometimes he forgot to eat until a persistent growling in his belly reminded him to pay more attention.

At the start of the class, when each student was told he was responsible for his own easel and supplies, Danzig summoned his nerve to approach Hoffman privately with a request for extra time to come up with the money. Hoffman studied him for a moment and then offered to pay him for cleaning up and stretching canvases. You'll learn more this way, he said.

When Danzig asked him how he could thank him, he shrugged and turned away. Just keep working, he said.

TONIGHT, HOFFMAN was in an especially dark mood. A sheet-covered cadaver was lying on a steel table in the middle of the studio, a room that was always kept cold but tonight felt even colder. Hoffman had promised that this would be the first of several classes devoted to drawing not from life but from death.

Danzig and his classmates knew only a few details about Hoffman's past, but tonight he seemed to want to talk—or, more accurately, he wanted to deliver a tirade about how many artists had been destroyed during the war, not just the obvious camp victims God knows but the ones whose work was deemed obscene and dangerous, the ones whose spirits were killed. The ones who could no longer create in such an atmosphere either went into exile or—Hoffman pounded on his own chest—simply stopped making art altogether.

Danzig's father, Walter, had often used the term "degenerate art," a phrase Hoffman used now with heavy sarcasm. And where were any of those so-called artists now, his father would mutter, and anyway when was this lazy son of his going to get serious about earning some money for the family; he was old enough to be paying rent and his share of the cost of food the way other grown children did.

Hoffman stood next to the table where the draped body was lying, and his pale face flamed red. He rubbed at the bridge of his nose and laughed bitterly at some private joke, turning toward his students but speaking to no one in particular.

I had a Jewish grandfather, you know, he said, as if continuing a conversation begun long ago.

He pointed to his bad left leg, the one that caused him a severe limp. Even beneath his clothing, it was possible to see that the right leg was far more developed, while the left one looked as if it belonged to a young boy. Hoffman had already told them that this was his reward for a childhood bout with polio, and they knew it had kept him out of the army and well away from the front lines.

Danzig's father would certainly have sneered at Hoffman for being not just a quarter-breed but also a coward and useless to the nation altogether. Needless to say, Walter would never for a moment consider the possibility that Hoffman had much more to offer than his body. He was perhaps the only teacher Danzig knew who passionately believed that art was as important as food, sometimes more important even, sometimes worth going hungry for.

And my mother killed herself, if you want to hear the worst of it, Hoffman added.

At this, Danzig felt as stunned as if Hoffman had been speaking to him alone, yet no one else seemed quite able to look at their teacher either. This was not what teachers did: reveal so much of their own histories, their emotions. Danzig realized he had never known anyone who admitted to a suicide in the family, even though there were stories of many after the war. There were so many secrets, so many unvisited graves. For the first time he realized that Hoffman always referred to his anatomy skeleton as Herr Doktor, and Danzig had never asked why.

For now, though, Hoffman's revelations were more than he could absorb, especially in the presence of this dead body. All eyes were on the white sheet, the unmistakable shape of a woman beneath it. Danzig felt an increasingly desperate urge to leave the room before she was unveiled.

Hoffman went on to say that he had ended up in an orphanage and should have been euthanized if the Nazis had had their way. It was worse than you can imagine, he said. You almost don't want to know that people are capable of these things, but they are.

At that point and without any further warning, he pulled the sheet halfway off the cadaver. He said, Here you go— your first dead body.

Danzig looked away immediately. This is my second dead body, he thought. And from the corner of his eye, he saw her.

White as porcelain, but with that gray-blue color infusing her skin, as if she were under ice.

He felt his knees weaken a little, and though he tried to lock them, they buckled even more. He forced a few deep breaths, nearly gagging on the odor of formaldehyde, and that was when he saw the fleck of nail polish on one of her fingernails. Bright pink, flaking off.

Hoffman was saying something about how they were not allowed to turn away. They had to face this truth of the body if they had any hope of being artists, if they had any chance of bringing their figures to life on the canvas. But there was nothing Danzig could do to keep himself in the room, to stop himself from leaping away from that terrible vision. He pushed past anyone who stood between him and the door. And he barely made it down the hall and into the bathroom before he began to vomit.

AFTERWARDS, HE LEFT THE BUILDING without returning to the classroom for his things. His footsteps echoed loudly in the empty hallways, and yet he was profoundly grateful that no one came after him. There was no way he could face his classmates, much less Hoffman. Bodies were all they had left, and Danzig had turned away from the truth.

Arriving at his parents' house, he looked through a back door window and saw his father at the dining room table with another man he didn't recognize at first, both of them looking grotesque in the dim light. From where Danzig stood, it appeared almost as a stage set, a play for two characters with a nearly empty bottle of whiskey between them on the lace-draped table. Although his mother was nowhere to be seen, Danzig imagined that she was hovering in the shadows, waiting as always to be summoned for service.

He was shivering from the cold; yet, the thought of going inside and inhaling that atmosphere seemed unbearable. When the man seated at the dining room table turned his head, Danzig saw that it was Mateus's father, the one who had almost thrown away his paintbrushes. Of course. He could tell by the gleam in their eyes that they were talking about the war again, reminiscing.

Both men laughed and toasted something by clinking glasses, spilling whiskey onto the tablecloth and then laughing all the more. The sounds chilled him further, and Danzig recalled Mateus confiding that his father had been tried at Nuremberg but eventually acquitted.

No wonder he felt so convinced that Mateus's house couldn't be any kind of refuge. Turning back toward the street, Danzig found himself entertaining a recurrent fantasy, the one in which he had his own apartment and a vast messy space to paint in. What a state of independence that would be.

But meanwhile? The only place he could think to return to was Hoffman's classroom. He had left his precious brushes behind and knew he had to go back. By this late hour, he hoped, all of the other students would have left. Maybe even Hoffman would be gone for the night, and Danzig could curl into some corner for sleep, wrapped in the coat that he'd left behind. He began to run, finding relief in the stretch of his legs, pulling deep breaths of frigid air into his lungs.

It wasn't until he had his key out and was aiming for the lock that he remembered the cadaver. This was why he'd run out into the cold in the first place. He jammed the key back into his pocket and almost shouted at himself in frustration. Inside, he saw Hoffman silhouetted in the hallway light, his face in profile and a hat in one hand. Too late to slink away now. Turning toward the door, Hoffman looked terrified for a moment, seeing only shadows.

Who's out there? he demanded.

It's just me, Danzig said, trying to step closer to the light of the doorway. I forgot my things, he said.

Hoffman opened the door and faced Danzig, urging him inside. You're without a coat?

Danzig hesitated, trying to see past Hoffman into the darkened classroom. He was still panting a bit from the run.

Just come back in, Hoffman said, and then he gripped Danzig by the elbow, pulling him across the threshold and closing the door. Don't worry, he added. She isn't here anymore.

Sure enough, the table and the draped body were gone.

No one left except Herr Doktor, Hoffman said. The skeleton was hanging in its usual place beside Hoffman's desk.

Danzig tried to laugh, but nothing came out. He felt his shame returning from earlier in the evening, imagined for a moment that he could smell his own vomit from the bathroom down the hallway.

I'm sorry, he mumbled. I tried to stay.

Never mind, Hoffman said. It's not so easy at first.

The longing rose up in him to tell his teacher everything: about Margot, about his father, about the dreams he'd had of flying across the ocean. But his words felt caught somewhere deep, blocked by the cage of his ribs.

Danzig pulled his hands out of his pockets and flexed his fingers to warm them, felt his legs stiffen into position as if he might not be able to rely on them to hold him upright. The residue of being so cold? No, something else. Fear.

Listen, Hoffman said. What are you doing on the street so late anyway? You should be home. In bed.

Danzig nodded, then half smiled. I don't think I could sleep.

Hoffman looked hard at him again, as though reading beneath his skin. I know that feeling, he said.

Can I stay here tonight? Danzig blurted. I just don't—

You don't have to tell me, Hoffman interrupted. I was your age once too, you know.

They exchanged a complicated look, and Hoffman reached down to rub at his shriveled leg, grimacing. The cold makes it ache, he said. He leaned heavily for a moment on Danzig's shoulder, then straightened and put his hat on his head.

You can always try talking with the Doktor, Hoffman said, his tone surprisingly serious. He knows a little something about dreams.

When the door opened, chilled air rushed inside with a vengeance. Danzig took a step back, wrapping his arms around himself. I'll lock up again after you, he said.

I know, Hoffman said, and he leaned forward to put his hand on Danzig's shoulder again. This time the grip was so merciless that Danzig could feel his teacher's fingers pressing on his bones.

Paint until dawn, Hoffman urged. If you're lucky, you'll leave yourself behind. He stepped outside and vanished quickly into the darkness.

Alone with the skeleton, Danzig turned to face the hanging man. When he closed his eyes, an image of the death's head insignia rose up, terribly white on a black background.

He pictured again the scene of his father at the dining room table with Mateus's father, their faces dark with pleasure. When he opened his eyes again, the skull's gaping sockets looked back at him without pity.

But what if it wasn't inescapable. What if he could get far enough away to forget his ghosts, or at least shrink them to a less nightmarish scale. He felt all of his muscles flex in preparation for this journey. Reaching toward the skeleton, he curved his fingers around its shoulder bone just the way Hoffman had gripped his. In his other hand, he held on to his brushes as if his life depended on them.

1953: Danzig

IT WAS HIS SEVENTH BIRTHDAY, but it began almost unnoticed, no one in the house pretending any happiness. Even before he got out of bed, listening for the sounds of his parents, Danzig could tell there was an especially dangerous mood in the air, his father slamming doors on his way out of the house.

Then, after he was gone and Mutti went down to the kitchen to bake a birthday cake, Danzig could tell from the way she leaned her weight against the kitchen counter and from the particular tilt of her head that she had probably been awake all night.

His older sister, Margot, was already out of the house, leaving without a word. He tried not to feel disappointed that she hadn't knocked on his door to wish him a happy birthday. His throat felt sore and tight from the effort not to cry. Mutti tried to make him feel special by promising Danzig he could have cream and some jam on his cake, but when he saw the fresh bruise at her cheekbone, he felt his heart squeezing like a fist. She was the one who needed comfort, but he didn't know how to give it.

He told her that what would make him feel best was permission to go for a walk by himself.

It was Saturday. Mutti packed him two hard-boiled eggs,

some bread, and a thermos with hot tea inside, placing everything in a small leather knapsack. His favorite route took
him through the quiet alleys of the neighborhood, and he
lingered as usual around the edges of the blasted remains of
an apartment building, still in ruins, all these years after the
bombs had hit. Most of the outer walls were obliterated, but
somehow the building still stood, with scenes of interrupted
life exposed to the elements.

He knew that Mutti planned her own walks to avoid this
place, but Danzig went out of his way to study it. For as long
as he could remember, this strange ruin had seemed to
Danzig an enormous closet full of ghosts. Furniture was still
arranged as if the owners had left abruptly but might return
at any moment. The wallpaper and at least one remaining
curtained window made him think of his own bedroom at
home. On the fourth floor, the top one, there was a room still
containing a sink and a bathtub, which he sometimes imagined must be full of rainwater or even snow, depending on
the season.

Recently Danzig had started carrying around a small
notebook in one of his back pockets, with a pencil for captur-
ing things that caught his eye. Trees at the end of winter, a
pile of what looked like bicycle parts, the expression on an
old woman's face while she stood in line waiting to buy vegetables at the market. Hidden under his mattress, he kept a
pile of pages covered with drawings of the bombed building,
room by room and from several angles. Sometimes he envisioned it from the perspective of the pigeons, flying overhead
and perching inside, no one to stop them from nesting in the
corners.

He did all of his sketching as secretively as he could, because even though his teacher had singled him out for his drawings, his father had gotten furious at the note she had sent home, with her suggestion that Danzig might have the makings of an artist.

What an absurd idea, his father had ranted. Useless and good for nothing practical, that's for sure.

He tore the note into shreds and stared out the living room window while Danzig fingered his pencil and made plans to hide all his drawings in a drawer at school from then on. He hoped the teacher would not try again to pay him extra attention.

School was already uncomfortable enough as it was, particularly in the form of a flurry of teasing involving Danzig's name. Several of his classmates made fun of his having the same name as a city, and who did he think he was, or was he a place for ships to come and go—a port, was that it—or maybe he was Polish and why didn't he go back where he came from.

This was something he never told his parents about, as if he knew without asking that this was not a subject to discuss. But then of course hardly anything was discussed in the family, his father angry about almost everything and his mother always sad, and not much spoken even at meals except requests for food to be passed across the table and always the reminders about how to use his fork properly and how not to put his elbows on the table and did he want people to think he was raised by farmers who lived in the country and didn't know any better?

ON ONE CORNER that he had come to think of as his personal property, Danzig found an old vegetable crate, which he turned upside down in order to sit for a while and eat his lunch. From there he could gaze at the bombed building and keep an eye on two streets and several directions at once.

That was how he saw Margot approaching from the distance; he recognized her dark blue jacket flapping unbuttoned and the shape of her legs as she walked. She was eighteen, almost a grown-up. Walking toward him, she kept her head down, so he waited to see what she would do when she got closer.

Margot didn't seem at all surprised to see her brother; in fact, the first thing she said was, I knew I would find you here.

You did?

Of course, she said. You come here all the time. I've watched you.

He moved over on the crate to make room for her and offered her a sip of tea from his thermos. She folded her coat beneath her, sat down, and pulled her bare knees close to her chest. Taking the small cup, she held it in both hands, breathing its aroma before taking a drink.

That tastes good, she said. Thank you.

Danzig apologized for having finished all of his lunch and having nothing else to share. But Margot didn't seem to mind. I'm not hungry, she said. And anyway, I'm here to give something to you. For your birthday.

So she had remembered after all. He couldn't help grinning at her, pleased for the first time since waking up. She didn't smile back, but still he felt warmed by her nearness; his sister had come all this way to find him and give him a birthday gift. When she told him to close his eyes and open his hands, he put the thermos onto the ground at his feet, and held his hands palms-up on his lap.

I want to tell you something, she said.

Danzig kept his hands open, expectantly, though he felt nothing yet. He wondered how long he should keep his eyes closed.

Margot took a deep breath and continued. It may not even make any sense to you now, or for a long time, but I want you to know that I'm going away.

Danzig's shoulders slumped involuntarily at the sound of her words, even though he had expected something like this all along. For some time now, Margot had stopped smiling. Not just at him but at anyone. She was so pretty and her hair was so blond it was almost white; she had a lovely light in her eyes. At least that was how she used to be.

He wanted to ask her where she was going, and when, but then he felt a small wooden box being placed in his hands, dense with the weight of its mysterious contents. Can I open my eyes now? he asked.

Go ahead, Margot said. And you can open the box too.

Danzig lifted the metal clasp and pulled up the lid, exposing three long-handled paintbrushes lying side by side, pale polished wood with dark horsehair bristles in various widths. He reached a careful finger toward the coarse ends, stroking them.

His sister had been watching him on his walks, so she knew about this too, about his secret life.

Margot removed one of the brushes from the box, the one with the smallest bristles, and she very gently touched Danzig's cheek with it.

It's okay, she said. I won't tell Papa or Mutti either.

He didn't know what to say, so he sat silently, watching the wind blow some of the dust around their feet. Margot's shoes were very muddy, and he wondered where she had been wandering. The pigeons cooed above their heads. Margot began talking again, but so softly he had to strain to hear her voice.

The worst of it is that you'll be left alone with them, and that you'll be trapped. I'm only comforted by the idea that you'll eventually find some way to escape, and it will be a better way than the path I'm taking, and it will be yours to discover.

Danzig listened so hard he almost stopped breathing. Margot's voice sounded as if it were coming from another room, somehow muffled and hoarse.

I'm out of choices, she said. And it's no one's fault.

She twisted her hands in her lap, and he noticed that her fingernails were bitten so far down they were almost invisible. He studied his own hands where they held tightly to the edge of the wooden box.

You don't know this, Margot went on, but I tried to stop you from being born. I was ill when Mutti was pregnant with you, and I made her so sick the doctors thought she would lose the baby. But she didn't. And you survived. When you came into the world, and Papa saw you were a boy, that was the most awful news to me, because it meant he would want to see himself in you, and that would start things all over again.

Margot sighed, and reached down to rub some of the dried mud off her left shoe. Danzig offered her some more of the tea from his thermos, but she shook her head.

Who knows how you'll turn out. Maybe it will all be fine in the end. But I want to ask you to remember me. Can you do that? Can you promise?

He felt as though she were asking something he didn't fully understand, and he almost imagined that if he said he would forget her, maybe she would stay. But that would mean she would remain unhappy, and he couldn't do that. She seemed to need this thing from him, this promise. So he nodded Yes.

At least you can try, she said. That will be enough.

DANZIG RETURNED HOME ALONE; Margot had explained she would be back very late, long after he was in bed. He made sure he had time before dinner to hide Margot's gift, clean himself up, and help Mutti set the table.

His father seemed even angrier than when he had left the house. He told Danzig to retrieve one of his dust-covered boxes from the basement, only to change his mind. He yelled when Danzig's clothes became dirty from moving the boxes around, barked at him to wash his hands three times, and then threatened to keep him from the dinner table all the same.

Mutti tried in her usual timid way to intercede. It's the child's birthday for once, she said, and the way she said "for once" made Danzig consider what a good idea it was to hope that next year everyone would forget his birthday entirely.

When his father at the cloth-covered dinner table said the

obligatory words of birthday wishes, Danzig didn't look at his face directly. He had learned that much from watching Margot, and seeing that if you could somehow stay out of his way, you could at least sometimes avoid being yelled at.

Still, his father always found ways of tormenting him, made sure that he was given jobs to do before he was allowed to eat his meal or play or read a book. He was inspected for cleanliness in the mornings before going to school, and he was sent to bed without food if he ever left a job half finished—or worse, if he said he had done something when actually he hadn't at all.

Mutti could not quite manage to defend him; he had learned that very quickly when he went to her for help. And of course Margot had done her best to keep out of sight altogether. Even before she started spending more and more time out of the house, she had been no use. He was on his own, and his father was the enemy, and it was all very clear and without alteration.

IN THE WEEKS LEADING UP to his birthday, Margot had been staying out practically all night, disappearing silently and reappearing just as silently, so that he never could be sure whether she was at home or out except for the small strip of light gleaming from underneath the door to her attic room. When the door was closed and the light was on, she was at home; she hated to sleep in the dark and always kept a small night-light burning beside her bed. But when she was out, the door was open, as if waiting for her to come back and close it again.

Danzig stayed up very late on the night of his birthday,

silently waiting for Margot to return so he could show her the drawing he had made after dinner. Having pretended to sleep while he waited for his parents to go to bed, he had pulled out his sketchbook and drawn his sister's face from memory, using moonlight to illuminate the white page. Something about her sadness that afternoon, about the way she looked off into the distance when she was talking to him—he wanted to see if he could capture it.

He was proud of the likeness and thought that if Margot liked it, maybe he would use it as the basis for a painting, his first one with the new brushes. He would paint her portrait and give it to her as a surprise. Maybe she would take it with her when she went away, but if he hadn't completed it before she left, he would find a way to send it to her. Or give it to her when he visited, wherever she was living by then.

Despite his best efforts, he must have fallen asleep. He woke up in the darkness and had to go to the bathroom, and he was puzzled to see that Margot's door was still open. There was no light inside except what was being sent by the moon through her window.

There used to be a time when she would let him sit up there in a window seat, where he could look out and see the street and the trees, the neighbor's houses, a pigeon or two on the roof next door. But that was before she started keeping the door closed when she was in and before she stopped smiling at him.

She was still out, although no one had said a word about her empty chair at the dinner table, as if saying her name aloud would make her absence more real. This way both her absence and the empty plate were invisible, imagined, except now Danzig knew that she was planning her escape.

Meanwhile, the door to her attic room was open, and the moonlight was spilling into the hallway. He paused there to listen for her breathing and heard only silence. For some reason, he whispered her name and then felt strange; something cold made the back of his neck shiver. He passed her open door without looking inside.

The bathroom was at the end of the hall. There was a faucet dripping, steadily making its one-note song. Fumbling with his pajamas, not even turning on the light, Danzig went inside, and that was when he saw Margot. In the bathtub, one hand dangling over the side, and her closed eyelids were violet, her fingernails indigo. Everywhere else her skin was not just white but pale blue, gray-blue, like the color of the sky before a storm.

1988, 1993: Merav

MERAV AND YOSSI sat in the shade of a rock wall, watching the heat shimmer just beyond them. Nearby, periodically kicking up small eruptions of chalky dust, Tzvi worked on a landscape, spreading paint with a palette knife as if preparing a meal. One of two adults in charge of the group of kibbutz teenagers, Tzvi was doing his best to ignore them, keeping his eyes on the view instead.

It was the first afternoon of a five-day desert hiking trip. In these hottest hours of the afternoon, the air was so parched that Merav felt her sweat evaporating before she could see it on her skin. She held her water bottle between her knees and tucked herself more solidly against the cool surface of limestone behind her back.

Merav was thirteen, Yossi a year older. Recently they had been experimenting with kissing, tentatively allowing the very tips of their tongues to meet inside their joined mouths. It was as if their bodies had begun some new form of conversation and the language didn't yet have much of a vocabulary. She imagined they were teaching each other a strange new grammar, making it up as they went.

While Yossi traced designs with his thumb on one of Merav's bare calves, she studied the textures on Tzvi's painting, thrilled and aching all at once. His translation of land and sky into something so viscous and malleable blurred with her newly rising desires, and she had to bite her lip to keep from exclaiming out loud. Holding her hands up and making a frame with her fingers, she tried to see what Tzvi saw, the subtle abstractions of sand dunes as blocks of light.

In his studio, she often watched him mix paints and work on huge wall-like canvases. But out here in the vastness of the desert, Tzvi squeezed acrylics directly from the tube onto the thin notebook-sized boards he had brought along. Raw umber and burnt sienna glistened in the bright sun and made Merav feel thirsty for everything.

Tzvi had fallen into the habit of spreading long sheets of blank paper on his studio floor for her to draw on, letting her find her way toward her own imagination. Paint would come next, he promised. But first she had to get comfortable with the whiteness underneath.

She could see that Yossi still had virtually no interest in Tzvi's artwork. He thought Tzvi was a little crazy, and several times he had told Merav not to visit him so much in his studio because she might get crazy too.

Maybe all those paint fumes are the reason, Yossi whispered, and he twirled his fingers beside his temples to suggest that Tzvi wasn't quite right in the head.

On this trip, as always, Merav and Yossi were inseparable, dark-eyed and wild-haired and perfectly matched in stride, their brown legs sun-baked and lean. They had been taking turns growing taller, sometimes Yossi just beyond her and sometimes the other way around, but mostly lining up to balance at their hip bones and shoulders. Both of them were the only children in their families, though it always felt as though they were surrounded by a crowd of siblings—this group on the trip, for example, rarely leaving them alone.

When Tzvi turned around from his painting and caught Merav and Yossi kissing, he laughed and winked at them. But then he pointed a wet brush at her, almost as if he wanted to deliver his message in vivid color.

Don't fall in love yet, he said. You've got greatness to find first, and paint doesn't like to be taken for granted.

Yossi nudged her in the ribs, tried to pull her face back toward his own so he could kiss her again.

And don't bother having children, Tzvi added, frowning, turning his back on them. Anyone can do that.

Merav tried not to listen too closely to either Tzvi or Yossi. At least she reminded herself that falling in love and having children and all the rest of it were her own business. Even her mother, Ilana, had begun to notice that Merav was not fond of being told what to do and was apparently learning to keep her mouth shut.

Maybe Ilana had been this way at her age too. As for having children, Ilana had raised her one daughter alone, which had always both pleased and terrified Merav: the idea that fathers didn't necessarily have to be in the picture beyond their original contribution. She had never known anything about her own father, not even his name.

Now Tzvi pointed with his brush at a moving cloud of dust in the distance, which turned out to be a family of Bedouins following the path of a dried riverbed, camels loaded with belongings. At the start of the trip, Tzvi had negotiated with a group of camel herders in what sounded to her like fluent Arabic. He said afterward that he had wanted them to know where their paths might cross.

As Merav watched, the figures entered Tzvi's painting as if in a dream, approaching a palm oasis that might have been real, might have been a mirage.

THAT NIGHT, she and Yossi lay awake under the stars, not the way they sometimes did on the kibbutz, on a wooden platform and with the sound of roosters to awaken them in the morning. Now they were in the middle of a moonscape, desert curves all around them like sleeping animals. After dinner cooked on an open fire, Tzvi told ghost stories late into the night, insisting they were true.

Yossi's erection was the first one Merav had ever touched with her hand, an experiment they conducted after everyone else was asleep. They lay with the unzipped edges of their sleeping bags side by side, opening toward each other like leaves. With trembling fingers, Yossi found his way inside her body, and she felt flooded with liquid exhilaration. He explored her the way she imagined a blind man might discover the world, mapping her with his fingertips, learning her landscape from the inside out.

Even with Yossi's mouth at her ear, she kept seeing Tzvi's paintings behind her closed eyes, the gleaming colors turning matte and thick under the heat of the sun. She loved the way the movements of his arms could be seen in the way the paint explained itself on his boards, the way the desert spoke through his body's language.

Yossi whispered something that sounded like a prayer, though none of the words sounded familiar. He was falling asleep. Merav wanted to drift away also but couldn't, too astonished by the infinity of stars overhead. Somewhere nearby, the ghost of the fire was still glowing. She stayed awake all night and discovered for the first time that the stars keep following their own paths across the bowl of sky, disappearing only temporarily behind the brightening curtain of day.

WHEN THEY SHOULDERED backpacks again in the morning, Tzvi promised them an oasis: complete with palm trees heavy with dates, and deep surprising wells of cold water. They hiked across wide expanses of sand, following the direction of his already vanished Bedouins, and the promise came true: no mirage but a real place held like a secret in the closed fist of the sand. All of them stood in amazement beside a pool surrounded by boulders, the air so cool it felt imagined.

Merav was the first to peel off her clothes and dive in, reveling in the relief on her dusty skin, the way her hair welcomed the drenching. She spun around, sending diamonds of drops flying in all directions. Yossi laughed, all his bright teeth showing, and she watched him strip to join her in the water, saw how he leaped and danced in eager anticipation.

Smiling at the sky overhead, at Tzvi who was already setting up for another painting, at the others from the kibbutz who seemed to her like young children, Merav remembered how Yossi had reached between her legs and how she had welcomed him. As if he belonged there.

FIVE YEARS AFTER THAT HIKING TRIP, Merav and Yossi crisscrossed the desert separately, members of the same army but never together the way they had once been, estranged by miles of sand and darkness. Sometimes she looked up at the night sky and imagined Yossi doing the same thing, their gazes meeting out in space, far from earth. They sent each other postcards infrequently, usually with a sentence or two at the most. Without being able to touch each other, they saw their words as pale and lifeless, fading ink on a dry stone.

When they were both back in the kibbutz on weekend leave, Yossi's neatly polished and unlaced boots sitting empty on his doorstep were the signal to Merav, just as hers were the signal to him.

Come see me. Spend the night in my bed.

SHE TOLD THE ARMY INDUCTION PERSONNEL that she did not want to be an officer. She had already made it clear many times. The pressure was intense: the kibbutz was so proud of its many offspring who had become officers, like Yossi, who surprised her by saying Yes of course he would be an officer when she'd been so certain they were the same about this too. They would never belong to that club; they would want to be free.

Yet he had found something in the army he wanted, even though it turned out that what he claimed he wanted was a chance to try to change things from the inside. At first she was deeply troubled, put off so completely that she wondered whether they could ever even discuss the subject.

Yossi seemed to love the sense of belonging and cama-raderie, the very things she had never quite loved even on the kibbutz and certainly not in the army. Merav was good at being likeable. She knew how to get along; she knew how to live with a group of women who gave one another just enough attention and solitude. Still, she wanted more time alone than she ever managed to find, and they all considered her rather distant and maybe even above it all, when in fact she just wanted a place in which to be quiet. The army was so noisy: the exercises and the dining halls and even the barracks in general. She longed for the silent maneuvers they sometimes practiced at night and especially the nights in the desert.

There was only one soldier in her unit with whom Merav felt something like kinship: a woman named Talia, who spoke very little and seemed like Merav to appreciate the desert in a very personal way. Talia had grown up on a kibbutz too. At night in the barracks, she hummed melodies that sounded almost mystical, but when Merav asked, Talia said she made them up; they were just things she felt pouring through her.

When I can't sleep, I find them in my head, Talia said. They come unannounced, and I can never make one up on purpose.

She smiled and closed her beautiful hazel eyes, as if the invisible music would find her only when she stood very still.

When Merav showed Talia pictures of herself with Yossi, Talia said she would have sworn they were brother and sister. Isn't it almost like looking into a mirror? she asked.

WEEKS INTO THE ARMY, months, and Merav still did not like to think of herself as a soldier. Studying maps and terrain, learning Arabic—these things kept her focused on being a student, expanding her mind, developing mysterious and underused regions of her brain in service to something outside herself, some higher good. But each time she was forced to remember that she was in fact a part of a military institution, a group whose purpose was to defend and when necessary to kill, everything broke down and felt unbearable.

She held her weapon the way she had been trained, but only in nightmares did she face the test and fail again and again. She could not shoot anyone, not to kill and not even to do harm. She couldn't imagine doing it no matter how many times she tried to conjure the image, the motive.

Once Yossi told her to think of someone aiming a gun at her heart, or at her mother's heart, but still her finger refused to pull the trigger. Her hands remained mute.

This was what she had tried to explain when she was inducted. No, she was not religious; that wasn't it. She simply had no desire to kill. She had no will to train herself, to overcome her resistance. She kept remembering her grandmother's story about the German soldier aiming a gun at her but deciding not to shoot.

She did not want to be able to kill, she told them.

Sometimes she imagined wearing her uniform inside out as a declaration of her refusal, some visible sign of her difference from all the others. Secretly she practiced ways of breaking the rules, keeping a button undone or a beret imperfectly placed, making her bed with asymmetrical folds. That meant that her record kept gathering stains of reprimand and insubordination, until she was actually on the verge of being dishonorably discharged.

This isn't a goddamned playground, her commanding officer growled. You aren't here to prove how clever and creative you are. Save that shit for the rest of your life.

Talia began telling Merav stories of a childhood visit to

the United States, in particular a trip to California that she had never forgotten. Redwood trees, as Talia described them, made Merav think of the reincarnated souls of giants. She imagined standing in one of the forests Talia told her about, leaning against the bark and listening for some unmistakable voice.

Talia said it was the opposite of the desert, full of damp shadows and fern groves. But it's quiet in the same mysterious way, she said.

LYING IN BED with Yossi before dawn, when the kibbutz was already in motion but not yet requiring their participation, Merav tried talking to him about the future. She told him about her struggles with her commanding officer and her hatred of the rules. What could possibly be so important about buttons, she wanted to know.

But Yossi was increasingly distracted, almost monosyllabic sometimes. They made love the way they always had, familiar and relaxed, but where they had once laughed there was now more silence, more thoughtfulness. When he told Merav he was going to stay in the army for another five years, the news stunned her into a long silence.

I'm going to art school, she said, surprising herself with the vehemence of her decision. She had only been considering it until then, but picturing Yossi with his gun and uniform, seeing her mother and her grandmother shaking their heads as they watched the news every night—all of it made her want to weep.

I want to create things, she said.

And I think that's why you need an army, Yossi said.

It made no real sense to her, but she had so little choice. The honor of the kibbutz seemed to be at stake, or at least that's what Ilana scolded her daughter with. The stories went around the dining room, Ilana said; everyone knew everyone's business. Merav noticed that Ilana's gray hairs were becoming more numerous, and all these years in the sun had left their mark on her skin. Esther's spine curved more and more like a question mark, though her grip was still fierce when Merav reached out to her.

Never rush a hug, Esther said. She held on and on, as if each embrace might be the last.

Merav decided to try harder to make it through the army without any more misbehavior, even minor infractions. She sharpened her salutes and worked seriously at obedience, aiming with genuine sincerity for a cleaner slate in her second and final year of duty. Her mother and grandmother had enough to worry about. This was merely the white paper, the background, she said to herself. The colors would come later when she was ready.

1996: Merav

ONE YEAR OUT OF THE ARMY, Merav was still getting used to being out of uniform. So it was especially strange to be standing at the Tel Aviv bus station with Yossi, who was in his uniform, and for some reason she wished he wasn't wearing it. She wished that they were back in the Sinai together, hiking the way they used to when they were teenagers. She wished they were moving backward in time instead of forward.

Yossi was trying to tell her something.

It was important; his eyes were gleaming with excitement over the significance of it all. They were leaning together against a graffiti-covered wall, trying to stay somewhere out of the way while all around them people were in motion, carrying bags and backpacks. Other soldiers shouted to one another and smoked too many cigarettes and got in each other's way.

The noise made it hard to think. Both of them were forced to shout, even when their faces were almost close enough to be touching.

Merav was trying to keep her full attention on Yossi, but for some reason she felt herself off balance, as if she were treading water and not quite managing to keep herself high enough above the surface to breathe.

Merav, he was saying. Merav, where are you? My bus is leaving soon, and we haven't finished talking yet. Merav, come back.

So she did. She came back. She tried to smile at him; she said I'm back, I'm right here, what is it?

He put one hand on her shoulder and said, You have to prepare yourself. You're going to have to see me wearing a tallis for once, a real prayer shawl, because Shoshana and I are getting married and her family is insisting on a religious wedding. It's all part of the big story for them, the whole package.

He tried to laugh, but of course he was serious and Merav had to pull herself up out of the water completely, although now she felt like someone drowning in the air.

She said, What are you talking about?

And Yossi said, Shoshana, that's what I'm talking about. Shoshana and I are getting married, it's going to happen soon, and now here's my bus, so we'll have to talk more next week when I'm back again. But please give me a sign in the meantime, a smile at least like you might almost mean it. Can you please try?

And she tried, she really did.

She made her face do something she hoped would look vaguely like a smile. She was imagining him standing beneath a wedding canopy, stepping on a glass, and she almost heard it shattering—or at least something inside her was breaking. Maybe it was the small bones in her ear; maybe that was what made her feel she couldn't quite keep her balance.

Yossi was kissing her on the cheek, scratching it with his half-beard, then getting onto the bus, and she was still attempting to remain standing there as if everything were all right.

They hadn't had time to meet for more than these few minutes at the bus station, because Yossi had been spending all of his leave with Shoshana. Merav realized with a small shock that it had already been a full year since she and Yossi had slept together, a year since they had decided it was time to stop being lovers. Hard to believe she had agreed to it, now, but on that dismal afternoon last February, lying together in his narrow bed while the rain pounded against the windows, they had discussed it, reasonably and sadly. Yossi had cradled her head on his chest, in that hollow at his shoulder where she fit so perfectly, and he had said they had to find new partners.

Merav felt the rise and fall of his rib cage as he took a deep breath and released it. Life is so big, he said.

When she held up one of her hands, he lifted one of his own and matched them, palm to palm, finger to finger. We grew up together, he said. But now we have to send each other into the world.

Silently, she practiced saying It's okay, it's okay, until she could almost believe it. Eventually she had turned her face upward to kiss him, just once, before climbing out of the bed to retrieve her clothes.

She told him he was right. It was time.

NOW, LEANING HARDER against the pockmarked wall of the bus station, she said to herself, This is the way it should be. Of course he was marrying someone other than her; even in the movies you didn't marry your best friend. Otherwise you would get along too well, and everyone knows a good marriage is full of fighting and then making up.

Shoshana wasn't even someone from their kibbutz; she was the sister of one of Yossi's buddies in the army, a woman he had known for months before Merav met her for the first time. She was the great-granddaughter of a famous rabbi. Her eyes were different colors, one brown and one blue, and Merav realized she had never before met anyone with eyes that didn't match. This seemed important somehow: the idea that Shoshana and her eyes were new pieces of the world Yossi had found for himself, exotic and a little disconcerting.

Yossi was on the bus and already seated somewhere. She couldn't even see his outline at any of the windows; it was too crowded and there were too many men in identical uniforms who could have been him.

SHE STOOD ON THE PLATFORM for several minutes after Yossi's bus pulled away in a brief cloud of exhaust. Her own local bus wasn't due for another half hour, which meant maybe she should take herself for a cup of coffee. She should move her legs and buy herself something sweet; yes, a pastry or a chocolate would help get rid of this bitter taste in her mouth. Something to make her blood travel in a different direction.

But for some reason she couldn't quite move. Replaying the conversation, she kept trying to recall more of what Yossi had told her about Shoshana and their plans. Yet all she could manage to think about was being in the desert, the Milky Way pouring across the blackness overhead, the scent of tea being brewed on an open fire.

Tzvi had given her one of his paintings from that trip, one

that she kept hanging on her bedroom wall. It reminded her of everything: the days when Tzvi taught her how to hold a paintbrush and how to memorize the play of light on a distant landscape, the days when she and Yossi crossed the threshold from teenager to adult. Now she no longer lived on the kibbutz, no longer visited Tzvi's studio. He was still there, still painting, his beard so long he looked like some biblical sage. She was in art school and Yossi was in the army, about to marry someone else.

Finally, though only a few moments had passed, Merav walked out of the station and saw the entrance to a small coffee shop, her bag pulling hard at one shoulder. Okay, she said aloud to no one. An espresso will help.

And that was when she heard the explosion, heard the wrenching of metal and shattering glass, the screams and the horns and the car alarms, all of it merging into a brutal cacophony. The sky was torn into something unrecognizable. Around the corner, just out of sight but close enough to send an evil cloud of smoke and debris, a bus ripped open.

Sirens went off all around her. Someone behind her in the café shouted God in heaven, not another one, and before there was anything else it was as if Merav felt an explosion in her own body where she felt everything seize, her heart and her lungs and even her blood.

Yossi's bus.

She collapsed. She actually fell down, and someone had to pick her up. She cut her knee and didn't notice the blood for hours, long after it had dried and turned nearly black. All she wanted was to stay on the ground, so at first she refused the help; she didn't want to rise.

Except that when she did get up, she had to command

herself to run, not away from the scene but toward it, because she had to know, she had to see it. She had to find him.

Later, many hours later, when she was with her mother, Ilana, watching television, brutal images of Palestinian houses being bulldozed, their walls crumbling in slow motion, and billowing clouds of debris rising up in ghostly protest, she listened past the sound of the machinery and heard what must have been the voices of women keening, mothers and wives shattered by grief.

Three months later, on Yom Hashoah, when the sirens wailed all across the country in remembrance of the Holocaust, that was when Merav made up her mind to leave. To her ears, the sirens wailed for Yossi this time, not for all the historical dead, of whom there were too many to count.

It was impossible for her to believe any of it. Impossible to stand still even for as little as two minutes without realizing that there was no way to remain frozen like this in the midst of such wailing.

Someone had imagined that it was possible to define space with sound, as if what was absent could be commemorated with silence framed by one grieving voice. As if body parts really were enough to identify a loved one. As if the empty places where your friends used to be could ever be reconciled. She was full of absence, and so was her country—at least it felt that way to her now. Ghosts hovered everywhere, and the living seemed intent on a relentless effort to placate them, as if that was what they knew the ghosts wanted.

She thought of the redwood trees Talia had told her about, the souls they had outlived and held inside them. They carried centuries in their towering cores, concentric circles of entire generations. Maps of lifetimes, memorized in a vertical and silent code.

It was not an answer or even the hope of finding one, but Merav understood that she would have to go away. She would have to pack as little as possible in order to arrive in a new country without much memory of anything. A kind of voluntary amnesia, that was her idea: to scatter the pages and start over.

THREE YEARS LATER, all the way in America, Merav would still find herself dreaming about walls being torn down, houses collapsing. In more than one nightmare, she was sorting through a mountain of rubble in search of Yossi's body, dreading what she would find but knowing she could not stop until she found something, anything, even a hand covered with so much dust it might have been part of an ancient statue. Cold and lifeless as stone, only more so.

She kept remembering how she had wanted to say something to let Yossi know she understood about the engagement and his choosing someone else. She wanted him to know she would find a way to live through it, but all she had said was *Mazel tov,* the same as a stranger would have said, the same as any stranger.

1942: Margot

WAS THERE a beginning?

Margot couldn't remember. There were Mutti and Papa; there was all of the shiny light bouncing off Papa's black boots; there was Mutti braiding her hair too tightly sometimes, pulling at her scalp until it ached and she wanted to scream, though she didn't. She never screamed.

She was a good girl and she obeyed them, always. She went to sleep when she was told, told only once, and she ate what she was given to eat, and she kept her room very clean, not a single thing out of place. Sometimes when she got out of bed in the morning she made it up so quickly it was as though no one had slept there at all.

Mutti and Papa whispered at night, just on the other side of the wall, but Margot willed herself not to listen because it wasn't right. She had her own privacy—at least she always thought so, until she found out her mother was reading her diary so that too wasn't her own. Nothing was, not even her own thoughts. A good girl would of course not have any thoughts too shameful to be shared; that was what Mutti told her, and the teachers said it too, they owed it to their parents. But more important even than that, they owed it to their country.

She was almost eight years old. She had her braids, so tight they hurt; she had her bright blue eyes exactly like her papa's eyes, her shiny face that he used to touch ever so briefly with the back of his hand and say he was proud of her. She was his good girl, his special one, and Mutti would smile and for a moment they were all happy and whole.

And Papa's shiny boots meant they were all doing the right things.

MAYBE THE BEGINNING was when Papa suddenly announced he was going to be sent to the east. He was leaving them for a while, and it was winter, and Mutti started knitting, knitting, not even stopping at night to sleep, it seemed. And no one was smiling even though it was all supposed to be a good thing.

Papa told her it would be all right, and she and Mutti were to take very good care of each other, and he would come home soon. Mutti told her not to cry, and the teachers said Germany was the strongest country in the world and history would record their strength forever and ever. Their time had come, the teachers said; it was a glorious time to be German and to witness such a triumph, to have a leader so perfectly designed for his time in history. They would all be able to tell their children and their children's children that they had been a part of it all, this rising like a phoenix from the ashes of the Great War and taking their rightful place at the center of the world.

In his study, Papa had a map of the world on his wall, outlining countries whose names she was just learning to pronounce. Once in a while he allowed her to watch the way he stuck little red flags to show where the soldiers were advancing, to show the wave of red growing larger. Later it was whispered that some were even going behind enemy lines, and one of her teachers assured them he knew how the special forces were conducting secret missions to turn the tide of the war. The Russians had no chance, he said, in the face of such superiority.

What would happen while Papa was away? Where would the flags be placed? Would he rearrange them when he returned?

It was winter in Stalingrad.

ALL DAY, Mutti was in a frenzy of laundry and ironing, scrubbing sheets and hanging them in the bitter wind of the courtyard, and Papa was locked away in his study, wouldn't even come out for supper.

When Mutti prepared a supper tray for Papa and Margot brought it to his study door, she knocked and waited very patiently until he accepted it not only in silence but without even looking at her. He didn't notice how pretty she was in her new white blouse, the braids still tight even at the end of the day, her cheeks flushed with expectation. He took the tray and closed the door, and she couldn't help feeling that she'd disappointed him; she wasn't worthy of his attention.

The fact was that there were so many distractions in the house she had been unable to tell anyone about her day at school. Lying in bed at night, trying not to hear Mutti and Papa on the other side of the wall, she thought about how perhaps this had been the first day of her real life, the true measure of everything that followed. She was in a kind of daze, her inner private self still trembling with the enormity of what had happened.

Anyway, she thought, maybe it was best she didn't talk about it. This way she could savor it as her own, keep it as a kind of private candle burning in her mind, at least for a while.

Perhaps if she had told, they wouldn't believe her.

IN SCHOOL, there had been a fever in the air, something electric, a palpable sense of some threshold being crossed. For much of the morning, Margot was with her group, the Jung-mädel, all wearing their special uniforms, admiring one another. On the playground they stood together practicing a new song because there was to be a parade that day, a visit to the school by someone so special and important that it was a secret.

Out of the corner of her eye, Margot saw that her best friend, Otto, was standing off to the side, apart from all the other children. He was reading a book and pretending not to care about anyone, but she knew him well enough to understand something was wrong.

She blushed to remember the day before, in biology class, when she had gone from thrilling at the talk of war and battles to realizing she couldn't bear the sight of blood. She had asked to be excused from the dissection experiments because the frog's skin looked too pale, too translucent to cut with a scalpel. She couldn't bear to slice into a living thing. Well, all right—it wasn't alive, but it had been, not long before, and it didn't ask to be a frog. She couldn't do it and didn't even want to be a witness.

The boys laughed, all of them except Otto, who looked at her and tightened his lips as if to say that he would have to bear it for both of them. He could hardly ask to be excused himself, being a boy and therefore expected not only to wield the knife but to enjoy it. The teacher said something about the frog's anatomy, about the thumb being larger on the male; that's how you knew what sex it was, and the boys all laughed. The girls blushed and giggled, the teacher frowned at all of them, and Margot left the room, leaving Otto behind to fend for himself.

Margotto, they called themselves in private, as if they were one person, though of course they looked like opposites: her eyes so light and his so dark, her blond hair nearly white and his almost black.

Later, this would be called history.

THEY WERE ON THE PLAYGROUND still practicing the song when the news came that their special visitor was going to be arriving very soon. This was to be another kind of beginning, she thought, a day that would be the most perfect happiness of her life, better by a thousand times than Papa's kindest look.

Her friends Ursula and Gudrun and Annette all stood side by side with their perfect white shirts and blue skirts and brown jackets. It was like being in a dream the way they all lined up and held their arms in the salute so proudly and with such devotion. Margot felt in every one of her muscles

a kind of trembling, almost like music, almost the way she remembered the tuning fork vibrating when she was allowed
to hold it to give her group the perfect note to start on.

He walked past and stopped for a moment. Really it happened so quickly, and yet in her mind it lasted forever.

He looked right at her.

He touched one of her braids, tugged on it for an instant,
and nodded as if to let her know how much she pleased him.
She thought of Mutti, the tight braiding all those times as if
she had known all along this day would come, this instant,
when he touched her braid and nodded.

Then he strode on, his boots shining like Papa's but perhaps even shinier, and she stood there, almost trembling
with joy.

And she thought, He touched me. He touched me. Me.

1998: Merav

ONE MORE MINUTE, Merav said.

She was modeling for a composition class, offering them her usual warning just near the end of her final pose. A low moan of complaint sounded in one corner of the room, immediately echoed by several other students. The teacher, an energetic gray-haired woman in her sixties, looked beseechingly at the model platform.

Could you last a bit longer? she asked.

Okay, Merav said. Five minutes. And in those extra few minutes, Merav's right foot fell asleep. She felt it disappear like a ghost limb, and when she stood up at last, her entire right leg collapsed beneath her as if she were someone who'd forgotten she had had an amputation. This had never happened to her before in a classroom. She crumpled all the way down in a slow-motion cascade, tried standing up a second time, and fell again, laughing at herself, half embarrassed and half surprised.

Most of the students didn't notice. They were on their way out the door, or talking, or turned away. Even the teacher, who might have come to the rescue, seemed to be no longer aware of the model. But one person was brave enough to offer Merav a hand, and she leaned on him for a minute, waiting for the fiery sensation of blood bringing her foot back to life.

He said his name was Gabe, and they looked into each other's eyes very quickly before looking away. She was naked, after all, and he was holding her hand, and somehow there was a kind of propriety to honor, an unasked-for intimacy to be resisted. She thanked him for his help and he said, No problem.

It was almost exactly two years since Yossi's death, and what astonished her was the echo of her falling, as if this were an omen, a story of death responded to with a story of life. She would find out later that Gabe had a flock of birds tattooed on his back, migrating as though his body were a landscape over which they passed. That seemed some kind of omen too, although even in retrospect she never quite deciphered it.

After Merav was dressed again, Gabe approached her a second time out in the hallway. Now she noticed more fully some of his details: dirty-blond hair cut short and bristly, the way his shoulders moved even when he was standing still, and most compelling of all, a scar at his eyebrow that interrupted the line, as if someone had erased it.

Are you all right now? he asked, pointing toward Merav's feet.

She nodded. Fully awake now, she said.

Good, he said. Under one arm he held a black portfolio, and strapped diagonally across his chest he had not one but two cameras. She was aware of heat rising in her face, and a racing pulse. Something about the way he was looking at her.

I'm a photographer, he said, pointing at the obvious

equipment. Do you work that way too? For the camera, I mean.

Merav liked the timbre of his voice, his bright blue eyes. She said she had rules that applied only to photographs, that it was a bit more complicated. She knew she had time. She needed the money. And she admitted only to herself that she wanted to look at him some more.

TWO WEEKS LATER she parked her pickup truck outside the studio he'd told her he shared with two other photographers on the southern edge of the city. Hunter's Point was a former army barracks converted into spaces rented out to artists. Merav felt a strange blend of amusement and discomfort there, as a former soldier herself, walking down hallways hung with collages and monoprints and etchings—all of it, including herself, pieces of the army being transformed into art. She studied her feet, clad in a pair of red sandals, and considered with a deep sigh of reassurance how far away she was from combat boots and the slamming sound they would have made against these hard floors.

Gabe's studio door was wide open, and she stood for a moment in the doorway, surveying his off-white walls and high ceilings with exposed air ducts. She appreciated the open space, the lifting upward. Stepping inside, she saw that Gabe had draped a series of sheets for backdrop, and he was arranging a group of spotlamps, designing the light. There were windows, but they'd been covered with butcher paper, blocking both the view in and the view out.

It's a great place, Merav said, turning and taking it all in. She studied Gabe from behind her violet-tinted sunglasses: his lean frame and sculpted arms, his blond hair cut so short she could see glimpses of his scalp, and the stubble on his cheeks, the way his legs pulled at his faded jeans, his work boots.

It's not all mine, he said, grinning at her and looking away again. But the others aren't here today. We take turns so we each have two days alone, and then we all share Sundays. It works.

He sounded a little nervous, and later he admitted he had been quite jumpy for the first hour or so, but Merav was mainly focused on getting herself comfortable and trying not to pick up on his edge. It was always a balancing act for her: to be sensitive to the mood of her clients, yet not to absorb them too deeply inside herself.

Everything was a potential source of information for her modeling, any books on the shelves or art on the walls or even the kinds of textures he liked on his floors or furniture. This space felt simple, spare, orderly. There was a small refrigerator in which, she later learned, he kept only film and bottled water. He didn't offer her anything to eat or drink, which for some reason made her feel relieved. This was not a date or even a visit. They were both here to do a job.

For perhaps the first time since Yossi's death, she felt a surprisingly powerful tug of attraction, a deep hum of expectation that made her skin prickle. She found herself imagining that Gabe would be a very precise lover, someone who would touch her in practiced ways, measuring her responses by way of shifts in breath and pulse, almost like a doctor.

Focus, she told herself. Focus on work.

She said to Gabe that they didn't have to talk or get acquainted; she wanted things to stay clear. She repeated her rules about photography; they were different from other art-work. No portraits of her face, no commercial use of the im-ages without her written permission.

Actually, I have a contract for you to sign, she told him, and pulled two sheets out of her bag. A copy for each of them. He read it twice, carefully, nodding.

Okay, he said. His signature, she noticed, was coiled tightly at the beginning, then opened out into a release. She added her own to both pages, an M as a wave, with its long reach to shore.

Gabe had told her to bring along some music, saying it would be good to have something she was sure she'd like, so she had some CDs in her bag along with her props.

Do you want these? she asked, holding up the music.

He asked if she wanted to choose the first one, to warm up with, so she picked "Tidal" by Fiona Apple. While he turned on the music, she stepped out of her clothes and waited.

She made sure not to look exactly at his face when he moved toward her, waving a light meter in her direction.

I need to read your light, he said.

Of course, she said.

Sometimes I like to work close, so I hope this doesn't bother you. And he did come very close, and she couldn't help it: she breathed in and smelled him.

She thought it was a clean smell, as if he'd been in the sun and wind, and the air that blew into his hair had some-how stayed there, keeping strands full of its movement. That was one of the things she would remember for a long time after they no longer lived together: the scent of his body. Even though she would be the one who left, even though she chose to walk away, she kept one of his T-shirts in the back of a dresser drawer to remind her that once upon a time, their bodies had wrapped around each other. And that she had loved him.

THE PHOTOS GABE TOOK of Merav that first day ended up on the walls of his apartment, which eventually became the apartment they shared. He said later that at the beginning he fell in love with her feet, which was where he aimed his light meter in that first moment of getting close.

He squatted down, and Merav saw the top of his head, the center point where his hair swirled into a perfect spiral. As if his thoughts had a precise magnetic pull inward. That turned out to be something she made up: the idea of everything being pulled inside of his mind, but at the time she couldn't have known that. All she knew was that the spiral seemed symbolic; it seemed like a message inviting her to explore his territory, to wander in it as if it were some kind of labyrinth.

The close-ups he wanted were closer than those of any artist who had approached her before. He aimed at her shoulder blades, the line of her hand on one hip, her toes and ankles. For that day, at least, she didn't know what he saw through his lens; she just trusted herself to do what she always did, which was to find her stillness and let him read her.

In the space behind her music Merav heard the click of Gabe's camera. She heard him sigh and say Yes, and wondered if he had found the thing he was looking for.

AFTER THE FIRST HOUR, after a break during which the two of them made small talk about the teachers and the other students at the Institute where they'd met, Gabe dragged over two large cloth bags from a corner of the room. They were the kind used to hold rice. One turned out to be full of smooth, black, coin-sized stones, as if someone had collected them from the bottom of a river. Gabe poured them in a commotion onto the floor, which he had covered with heavy white paper.

I'd like you to lie down on these, he said. His voice sounded polite, but he was clearly not inviting a discussion.

All right, Merav said. She found they were cool and a bit slippery, uncomfortable at first. And yet once she relaxed, they had a lovely, sensual texture. She was reminded of a stony beach from years earlier, on a trip to the Greek island of Crete, a time when she had lain at the edge of the Mediterranean and allowed it to gently rock her back and forth. Closing her eyes, Merav imagined she could hear the surf. Gabe aimed his camera and kept clicking.

But it was the next part of the session that Merav would remember the most clearly. Gabe used a large stiff broom to sweep away the stones, making the white paper clean again. He lifted the other bag and began to pour out its contents: flour. It sifted down in clouds of pale smoke, pouring white on white. He laughed a little as some of it floated up and began to coat his face. His eyelashes and eyebrows turned white, and Merav laughed too. For a moment he could have been a child playing in a big sandbox.

But of course the sandbox was for her to play in. Gabe

went to grab a rag to wipe the flour from his face; he needed to be clean enough for the camera.

Just do whatever you want, he said. Just have fun.

The flour was so soft that Merav's feet sank into it as if they were plunging into surf. But it wasn't deep enough to let her feet disappear; it was just enough to cover her soles and up between her toes. Then she reached down to get it onto her hands too, to spread it onto her arms and legs as if she were splashing herself at the edge of the sea, to rinse herself with it.

The fine flour streaked her skin, felt like silk ribbons. She powdered her body, sprinkled and smeared herself, and then lay down completely, pulling handfuls of it onto herself like the softest of blankets. She might have been reenacting a tribal ritual, some act of worship.

Gabe didn't say a word but just kept reloading the camera when he used up a roll of film, and he continued shooting. For a little while, Merav imagined that Gabe was touching her with his own flour-covered hands, but gradually she nearly forgot he was there and lost herself in the dream she was having. Stones, sand, water, silk. She kept her eyes closed and submerged.

THEY DIDN'T MAKE LOVE THAT DAY, didn't actually touch. But it was all there between them: the electricity, the messages sent from skin to skin. Gabe stayed behind the camera and Merav stayed inside her silence; they both remained professional until the end.

But the following week when they met again at the door

of his studio, she knew something had shifted. For the first time she decided to break her own rules about sleeping with one of her clients.

I dreamed about you last night, Gabe said. I was dreaming in red light.

He told her it happened sometimes, when he was spending so much time in the darkroom he forgot to take breaks and get back into daylight. He said he stayed in there for hours, not even noticing that time was passing. She listened as he talked about the baths of chemicals, the laundry line of dripping prints, the concentration and anticipation.

It amazes me every time, he said. The images are inside my camera, on that tightly wound roll of film, and no microscope in the world can detect them yet. They're there, but they're invisible. I have to bring them all the way to life. Like magic.

Merav thought of herself rising into the air dripping like a shipwreck, an apparition, coming to life on a blank page hanging in a room of red light. She wondered for a brief moment whether she was giving herself away somehow, the way the Bedouins she met in the desert felt about their images being stolen and taken prisoner.

Gabe told her he was color-blind, so then she realized that even in his dreams red light wasn't exactly red. More like amber, he explained, or sepia maybe. But there were advantages. He said that seeing things in black and white was sharper and more vivid, more nuanced, than what he imagined other people saw.

There's an island somewhere whose inhabitants are almost all color-blind, he said to Merav. They weave incredible black-and-white rugs, full of detail and subtlety. People with ordinary sight can't even really appreciate them.

He was right; she couldn't quite imagine how he saw the world. His photos told stories about texture, shape, design. She wondered whether he might be able to teach her something she'd been trying to learn in the desert: how to see beneath the surfaces of things.

In the far corner of the studio, Gabe had spread out an array of photos to show her, the ones he had taken the week before.

Look, he said.

Image by image, Merav saw herself in pieces, saw how Gabe's camera had explored her. When she saw the flour like ashes on her skin, as though she were made of crumbling marble, she thought of a line from Leonard Cohen: "Let me see your beauty broken down."

For a moment, she felt stunned by the idea that maybe he was dismantling her, maybe he would never be able to see her whole. But right away she shook herself free of that idea, told herself she was only inventing fears to keep from falling in love with him.

This is how beautiful you are, he said. This, and this, and this.

He kissed the back of her neck, making her skin shiver all the way down her spine. The falling continued. Later, when they climbed into his bed together and he stared with such intensity at her breasts, she thought surely he was seeing into her heart. She imagined him seeing her even more intimately than his camera could: her beauty up close, her textures and lines, the temperature of her skin. She thought she could feel him absorbing every detail of her body, as if he were trying to memorize her, using the lens of his naked eye to record her naked image.

WITHIN MONTHS they decided to live together, then marry. Part of the urgency was logistical: her visa was expiring, and it all seemed such an obvious way to make that problem go away. They married at City Hall, handing flowers into the arms of strangers they passed on the steps outside. One of Gabe's studio partners offered to take photos, and for once Gabe turned up inside someone else's frame.

Merav wrote to Ilana after the wedding was over, assuring her it was nothing she needed to feel sad about having missed.

We are taking good care of each other, she wrote. And you'll meet him as soon as you come for a visit. Okay? Will you?

She knew Ilana hated to fly but hoped that somehow her mother would make the trip anyway. The redwoods were even more astonishing than Talia had led her to expect. She wanted a chance to show them to Ilana, to explain that even as the desert lived in her bones, she could grow roots here too. Gabe said that maybe in the winter they could visit Israel, float in the Dead Sea and take mud baths.

I've always wanted to see a kibbutz, he said. He pronounced the word with the emphasis on the first syllable, and Merav hesitated before correcting him. What would the desert look like to his color-blind eyes? Would he see nuances in black and white that she had somehow missed all of her life?

EVENTUALLY, THOUGH, she began to question the ferocity of his gaze. She thought he was aiming for her core, trying to climb all the way into her bones and then deeper still, reaching beyond the limits of the body. When they made love he kept his eyes open; he stared and stared. After a while she wondered, what did he see?

Although it took her some time to admit it, Merav began to sense that her body was only a receptacle for his desire, while her own desire floated elsewhere, in another dimension, invisible even to herself. They half-jokingly referred to these times as Letting Him Have His Way With Her, as if she were consenting to the use of her body, lending it out.

She told herself that she must still be grieving for Yossi and that Gabe would be her remedy in time.

Meanwhile, he stared at her breasts with so much hunger and compulsion it was as if she owned something he wanted to steal. She imagined herself sometimes as a painting, a photograph, a sculpture without an inhabited soul. Gabe didn't even seem to notice whether or not she was present there too, whether they were sharing the experience, joining somewhere in the meeting of their bodies.

He took his pleasure; in the end she could see it so clearly. Did he think that was a kind of giving? Maybe. But what was she giving to him? Permission to be taken? Finally, she stopped asking why it was enough for him and began asking why it was enough for her.

His photos began getting smaller while the white linen mats around them kept getting larger, surrounding his images with more and more white space. Merav envisioned herself shrinking inside a vast blizzard and dreamed about Gabe building a house with empty rooms, windows too high to look out from. He said he framed things, people, so that he could make them more visible, believing even as he cut off its edges that he was making a thing more real, more seeable. She started wearing clothes in all the colors he couldn't see, to camouflage herself in his landscape, disappear in front of his eyes.

The walls of their apartment showed a collection of Merav in parts, close-ups of her feet, hands, hip bones, shoulder blades. The one exception lay in a single photo that showed her entire, taken from behind her back. In a wide-open field stood a wooden picture frame the size of a doorway, balancing upright as if by magic in the middle of nothing. And Merav was walking through it, her arms held out to her sides, her fingertips just brushing the edges of the frame. She was stepping out of it and walking away.

1953: Margot

MARGOT STOOD at the kitchen sink in the very early morning before anyone else was awake, humming into the quiet. She peeled an apple in one continuous spiral, the same way her mother did and probably her grandmother had before her, their hands following the identical motions as if time were as continuous as the skin of the fruit. But then without warning came a terrifying thought, the kind she had been having so often lately, about all that she had inside of her, everything that had ever happened to her growing like weeds under her skin.

If she carried inside her these same gestures and echoing sounds, then it also stood to reason that she carried the coded messages of her father's life too. She carried his core inside her own.

Mutti said only that Papa had shadows the way everyone did. Where there was light there also had to be shadows, she said. But that meant Margot therefore had to live knowing that if she had his blue eyes and blond hair she must also have at least some of his heart, that frozen place inside where it should have been warm.

School—the place that had once upon a time been her heaven, her sanctuary—school had become impossible, yet another realm where everything was false and despicable.

Even the teachers who promised to tell the truth were always too cowardly to actually face it, to look into the mirror of the past.

Professor Mannheim showed them a film about the camps, except that he didn't speak or explain but simply spent the entire hour bombarding Margot's class with images in total silence. And when the bell rang, they went to the next class to learn about calculus or literature, and there was no room for them to think or take it in. They were all supposed to swallow it and carry on to the next lesson, because no one knew how to speak about it. No one.

What to say to the girls who whispered at lunchtime about their fathers returning from the front with frostbitten toes and missing limbs?

What to say to the boy in her class who told her that in his attic his grandfather had a copy of *Mein Kampf* that was bound with skin from a human back? He threatened to show it to her. He wanted her to touch it, and she said she would never. Never.

But was it any different that in her basement she knew there were medals of iron with her father's name on them? Those photos of Papa in uniform, and the photo of her in those perfect braids, and that certificate. All of it in unmarked boxes down in the dark, and who knows how many more secrets. And those boots.

History class was the biggest lie of all. They kept starting over at the Ice Age, when what she wanted to know, needed to know, was the history that had made her, not the rocks and rivers and trees. She wanted to understand how she could have fallen for it, how she could have become such a believer. How all of them had.

And because school wouldn't help her, she tried by herself to remember all the way back to the time before: before the trials, before the accusations, before the bombs. Back to the parades? The cheering and waving? No. Before that too. Before the war, before she was in school. Back to being held, being strolled around town. Being held on Papa's roomy lap, and *hoppe hoppe Reiter*. His scratchy wool coat, his hat, the cold air that always rushed into the house when he entered it, the outside carried in between his neck and his collar. How she reached into his pockets to see whether he had brought her anything. Secrets. Surprises.

The biggest secret of all, the biggest surprise. The enemy was not out there: it was inside all of them. The enemy was her own heart, pounding with joy at having been chosen. The one who got to be touched.

Back then she had held the memory of it like a talisman, especially after Danzig was born, as if this was the way she could console herself for being suddenly the forgotten child, the one who was no longer at the center. She felt sometimes that she could have wandered into the street, into the countryside, and days would pass before Papa and Mutti would notice her absence. She felt invisible, and for a while at least, the memory of being touched kept her alive, kept her believing that she mattered, that she was real.

PAPA COULD NOT find a position. He was classified in the category of Black, farthest from the acceptable White. Not even Gray, not even questionable. No. He had been too high up, too close to the inner circles. For those first few years it was all coming out, more clearly every day. Names on lists were being circulated among all the authorities. Her father was Black, the worst kind.

And so, out of necessity, her mother found work. Mutti had swallowed what little was left of her pride and gone in search of any position she could find, ending up as a seamstress. Everyone was trying to make old clothing last longer, not be so quick to replace old with new when after all, good wool ought to endure. Her mother was in demand. Though even with her, there was gossip; there were people who wouldn't let her do their sewing because of what came out about her husband. As if they were all so innocent themselves. They all swore that they were the ones who had kept their hands clean.

Margot looked at her hands in the kitchen sink and at the apple, which now had no skin. She remembered her reluctance to touch Danzig as a baby. Because she didn't want to pass on the stain she carried.

Danzig was too young to notice he'd been born into a new world; it was the only one he could know. No memory of the Before to haunt him because he was After. She envied him a little for that, but mostly because he seemed to stand for the new beginning of her parents' lives, whereas she was the living proof of some other vision they'd had. Danzig too was blond and blue-eyed, but the idea of his perfection she now heard about only in a whisper. It wasn't supposed to be said out loud anymore, even though Margot and virtually all of her schoolmates were the blond and blue. One day proud and the next—well, what?

————

SHE TOOK SMALL BITES of the apple, barely tasting it because of the dryness that came into her mouth every time she summoned more of the memories. Today she was going to revisit the whole story, and then no more. She was going to force herself for the last time to walk past the apartment building, the one that Otto used to live in with his family. The place where she and her best friend had explored each other's childhood bodies, getting to know the precise and mysterious texture of another person. She sat at the kitchen table, making her hands hold each other on the cool surface.

When she heard about the lamp shades made out of skin, she couldn't stop thinking about Otto, how beautiful and nearly translucent his skin seemed to her.

She made herself remember. Otto's much older brother had been arrested in the middle of the night, and the rumors spread that he was caught listening to the wrong radio station, seen distributing subversive leaflets. Several days later a sealed coffin was returned to the apartment. He had been tortured.

First there was talk of sending Otto out of the country, just him, and for a little while. A secret, he said. No one was meant to know except the close relatives, but of course he had to tell her; she was his best friend and he could trust her to keep a secret. He could.

Klara Stein's entire family had disappeared, and there were stories of entire families being loaded onto the backs of trucks, never to be seen or heard from again. But meanwhile her other friends, Ursula and Annette and Gudrun, were all like her: they joined the Jungmädel right away, delighted by their new brown jackets and dark blue skirts and dazzling white shirts. Otto said suddenly that his whole family was preparing to leave, fleeing to Argentina, but then he looked away. Maybe somewhere else, he said.

This time he was not allowed to tell her; she was in the Jungmädel, and she could not be trusted. He would no longer look her in the eye.

And then in a day, it was all over: his family's apartment stood empty; even the maid didn't answer the door, although from the outside it all looked the same. After a month had passed, Margot saw an officer's family moving in. They had claimed it as state property, someone said.

Margotto gone forever.

In school, there were more lessons about what they called racial science, more lecturing about degenerate art. The intended messages were increasingly clear: to be proud of certain things, disgusted and ashamed of others. Full of hatred and violence. Like Kristallnacht, when she was too young to remember, like the book burning she had heard about. The Jewish names turning into ash and floating up into the night sky.

MUTTI WOULD BE waking up soon, and Papa too. Margot quietly gathered her bag, the special package she had prepared for Danzig's birthday. And on the way to find him, she would make herself remember even more: how it all came crashing down, the bombing followed by the silences, the hunger and overwhelming disappointment.

Not right away. At first it was just a new reality to awaken to, the putting away of the uniforms, the disappearance of that salute, those words.

The erasure of the chalk-mark outlines of her other life.

And in her own family: the aftermath included the arrival of Danzig, as if they wanted to start their family over again. This made her feel even more as if her life was a mistake and had to be canceled. Mutti stroked the baby's soft head instead of paying attention to Margot; she stopped braiding her daughter's hair.

If Margot ran away it would only partially unravel her life, because she'd already tried once, and her father had found her, brought her back, locked her in one of the attic rooms as if to prove he was the only one to decide her fate.

Wouldn't it be ironic, in the end, if Danzig grew up hating them too? She would almost want to live to see that, almost. She would have to content herself with imagining it: their perfect son turning out to be a knife in their hearts, someone who could deny them any forgiveness or consolation.

She imagined Danzig ashamed, but perhaps not as much as she was herself. He wouldn't remember her. That was unlikely, except if he turned out to be the one to find her body; maybe that would stay with him forever. But she didn't want to hurt him; he hadn't done anything except be born to these hateful people, and it was sad to have to cause him pain. But it would mean that a memory of her would be kept alive somewhere.

Maybe Otto would paint his memory of her someday in a faraway city on some distant continent. Maybe that's how she would be resurrected. She tried to reassure herself that Otto had reinvented himself in a new country with a new name and a new vocabulary. Whereas Margot felt she would never be able to start over as long as she carried the same skin, the same bones.

Now she had to force herself to walk past it: the apartment house where Otto's family had lived and where his father's art studio had been. All the outer walls ripped away to reveal the abandoned interior: the table with chairs, the cabinets full of dishes, the bookcases half full, pictures hanging askew on the walls. As if waiting for them to return and resume their lives.

The dirt that would never wash off, the past clinging like an odor.

She thought suddenly of the courting dance of swans she and Otto together had seen once in the zoo: how the swans faced each other and turned in perfect synchrony, circling until they faced each other again and again.

Sometimes in her dreams, she saved him; she kept them all from disappearing. But in the end it didn't matter; none of it did. She had had no choice in this lifetime, and probably she had no choice about the next one. Just to start over anywhere, wipe everything clean, like someone trying to burn away fingerprints and erase them from the skin. To be untraceable somehow. A blankness, an empty canvas.

LATER, AFTER GIVING DANZIG the gift of the brushes, after trying to tell him as much as she could without telling too much, she spent hours walking in the falling light, hours making herself colder and colder, numb.

Until finally, in the darkest hour of the night, she returned to the silent, sleeping house and sat in her window seat for the last time. It was so cold outside and so warm inside, but not in her heart, not where she wanted to feel things.

She looked at her reflection in the dark glass, breathing on it to make a foggy background, and with one trembling finger she wrote her name on the window. She wrote it where no one would ever see it. MARGOT.

Then she wiped it away, one letter at a time, crossing herself out, until nothing was left but M.

The last mark. Until it too disappeared.

Part Three

The Present

MERAV WAKES UP filled with misgivings. It takes her several moments to shake off the vague residue of her dreams and locate herself in bed at home. She waits another few seconds to decipher the time of morning from the quality of the light and finally to remember what day of the week it is. Tuesday. The day she has agreed to drive out to Danzig's studio in Point Reyes.

Showering slowly, dressing carefully, she broods over her decision, sensing regret in the weight of her legs, the way she feels rooted to the floor. It's the opposite of the way she feels in water, this reluctant submission to gravity, and she keeps looking at the telephone, tempted over and over to make the cancellation call.

Steady, she tells herself. As if calming a wild animal.

IN HER PICKUP, driving north across the Golden Gate Bridge and into Marin county, she grips the steering wheel with both hands and keeps her gaze straight ahead. A wet film gathers on the windshield. Crossing water she cannot see because of the fog, crossing toward hills bathed in thick gray mist, she actually has to turn her wipers on as if it's raining. This is summer in the form of a blanket, a barrier as dense and threatening as a bad dream. The desert she carries in her bones is still astonished by the moisture of the atmosphere here, the shock of it in her skin and hair.

With each passing mile she feels increasingly haunted by the idea that this journey is a mistake. Her body hesitates at every exit, her foot briefly lifting off the gas, and yet somehow she keeps resisting the urge to turn around, even with the drumbeat in her head. It's Esther's voice, with Ilana too, both of them warning that she should be more careful.

You shouldn't be working for a German, they say. You shouldn't trust him, shouldn't be alone with him in his studio.

And taking off your clothes? Are you out of your mind?

Merav silently talks back to them. Hadn't Esther once grudgingly admitted it was possible there had been a few good Germans? That soldier—wasn't he deserving of credit for saving her life?

It's just there were never enough of the good ones, Esther would retort. Here she would lift her hands in a gesture of weary disgust, having reached once again the point in her story where the ending always turned out the same.

NORTH ON 101, the highway spreads out and is flanked by a hundred shades of green. Suddenly the fog seems to be changing its mind, pulling back the covers. Merav exits to follow Lucas Valley Road as it heads west, winding past bleached hillsides and developments that soon give way to hiking trails and ranches. The curves of the asphalt distract her for a while, and turkey vultures turn high circles, tearing blue openings overhead.

As the city disappears behind her back Merav recalls the transition from Tel Aviv to the kibbutz, the crossing from city streets to earth. When she rolls down her windows and feels the rush of cold fresh air stinging her face, she knows that this is exactly what she needs to be doing, even if her doubts stay with her like a passenger in the truck.

Steady on, she says out loud.

Passing through the almost invisible town of Nicasio, Merav catches her first glimpses of the mountain she has heard called Black Mountain by its owners and Elephant Mountain by most of the locals. It does seem to her to have an animal body, folds of shadows like wrinkles. She loves the way it lies there, imagining how it must look against the changing sky. Out of habit she begins to estimate its measurements, plotting its shape on a topographical map.

She thinks of that Hemingway story "Hills Like White Elephants," the one about an abortion except that the abortion never gets mentioned. Merav had read it in an English class at a local community college; she had briefly taken the class as a new arrival in search of improvements in her command of the language, wanting to be more fluent. Her Israeli accent softened, though not entirely.

The teacher seemed to like her, gave her A's, and asked to keep copies of two of her best essays, including the one on Hemingway. She had written about how the landscape in the story was the most memorable character, not just because it was in the title and used so symbolically but because it was what made her reflect on the resonance of geography in her own life. The desert had been so full of stories, the shapes rising in the dark, the sky so close and so far away.

Merav didn't take any more classes after that one. She

read on her own, visiting the public library once or twice a week to fill herself up. She sat in the art section of libraries and bookstores, turning pages, memorizing poses. She was learning how to believe in her invented American life, her changing understanding of who she could become in a country that wasn't exactly her own.

Esther had always called Israel her adopted mother, the one who embraced her after the war. They wanted to kill me, Esther said. And when I survived, I knew I had to get out of Europe for good.

For Merav it was all turned around. Exile was her choice to get away from being the one meant to kill, and she had wandered away from home in search of some other place. Meanwhile, she carried an uncertain identity with her. Did country live inside or outside, she wanted to know.

When she married Gabe, she married an American, but of course that didn't make her one, any more than obtaining a driver's license or a mailing address. She wasn't sure what it meant to be an Israeli, not if she no longer lived there and not if she thought she might never live there again.

Visiting Israel just after her divorce from Gabe, visiting her mother, made her feel more than anything like a stranger. She had "descended" when she left her country; that was the word they used. Her old friends accused her of no longer understanding them, and in a way they were right: she had begun to see their life from a distance, across an ocean and a continent too. Even Ilana accused her of not knowing any longer what it was like to live under siege.

Merav visited the cemetery where Yossi's remains had been buried, stunned by the waves of grief that shook her as she stood by his grave. The idea that his body was in pieces under the ground made her want to lie down and weep. She felt as if she too had been blown apart and never quite reassembled. Could it be possible that beneath her skin she still held some of his molecules? Could something they had shared still belong to her, even now?

THE SCRIBBLED DIRECTIONS steer her just around the outskirts of the town of Point Reyes Station until she pulls into Danzig's driveway. It is marked by windblown Monterey pines, amazingly expressive trees that Merav remembers noticing when she first arrived in San Francisco. They are all over Golden Gate Park, the fog blowing them into shapes that make each one seem inhabited by an ecstatic dancer.

The barn in front of her has an appealing weather-beaten softness, its wood faded to a kind of silver. She touches the door before knocking on it, feeling its furry texture on her fingertips. She takes a deep breath.

HAVING WAKED UP much too early, Danzig has been waiting for her for hours, distracting himself with extra coffee and even a spontaneous walk into town. The woman behind the counter at the bakery seemed surprised by his entrance, glancing at the clock when he asked for a baguette and two croissants. He thought he detected similar reactions at the market across the street when he bought five oranges and some absurdly expensive cheese, but maybe he was imagining it.

In his studio he rearranged the model platform several times, dusting off the space heater, which sadly had been out of use for a long time. He readied his neglected easel with stacks of clean paper and a fresh box of charcoal twigs, also black ink and some Japanese calligraphy brushes. Deliberately, he forced himself not even to think about setting out paints. If he listened, the canvases seemed to mutter in a chorus of dark foreboding.

Just drawings, he said to himself. Just that much.

Brandishing a broom with green handprints all over its handle, he swept the studio floor, nudging whatever accumulated out the front door and into the open. A breeze picked up the dust and sent it flying. For a moment, he pictured himself as a classic village shopkeeper—an image held from his childhood, from his long-lost other life. The silence of the morning soothed at least some of his nerves, though he couldn't help worrying that she might not come. She could disappoint him. Disappear.

WHILE MAKING a second pot of coffee he hears the sounds of her arrival: tires in gravel, an engine ticking into silence. And she is here, knocking.

Ending his tentative sense of calm, his heart practically bangs its own reply, and he has to remind himself that this is what he wanted. After no models for so many years, after nothing but those white canvases challenging him even with their backs turned, here is a possibility about to open.

WHEN DANZIG STANDS in the barn doorway, Merav is newly struck by the extreme paleness of his blue eyes, as though she'd forgotten him from seeing him in the classroom just over a week ago. He has what looks like flecks of gesso in his coarse gray-blond hair. His denim shirt hangs open over a moss-green T-shirt and a pair of well-worn jeans streaked and splattered with dried paint. There is a smudge of charcoal above his eyebrows, which are startled upward when he sees her.

Am I early? she says.

Probably not, he says, holding up a wrist with no watch. He opens the door wider to let her inside, and passing that close to him she smells turpentine and soap.

He is relieved nearly to the point of speechlessness to have her in such proximity again. The fresh air seems to follow her inside the studio.

He points her to a corner where there is a sagging overstuffed chair and a low wooden table. For your things, he says.

He moves toward a long stainless steel counter along one wall and holds up a coffeepot; it's splattered with paint like everything else.

You want coffee?

No thanks, she says.

Danzig watches her in his peripheral vision as she surveys the studio, taking it in so carefully that he wonders what she notices, wishes she would narrate for him. Why should he care what she thinks? He just does. She smiles a little as she does a slow turn, exploring.

The space is vast, full of diffuse light coming in from windows higher than eye level on all four sides. There are so many stretched canvases leaning against several walls that she finds herself counting them. Twenty-four. But they're all turned away; Merav can't make out whether they are blank or completed work or something in between. In a far corner, draped with sheets, she sees what appears to be a bathtub. There are unstained pine shelves upheld by brackets, covered with an array of cans and jars and bottles holding bouquets of brushes in all sizes and conditions, also various-sized palette knives, twigs, broomheads, and scraps of wood.

The floor is partially tarp-covered, with some smoothly worn boards showing through here and there. High beams crossing the ceiling look old and beautiful, massive as tree trunks, which of course they must have been when they were alive. Merav can see the deep green of the pines beyond the windows, and patches of blue sky. The fog could be either coming or going; she cannot tell.

The studio is cold, but a portable heater has been considerately placed near the model platform, which is braced against one wall and strewn with various batik-printed pillows and what look like old velvet and corduroy couch cushions. Merav pulls some soft cotton fabric out of her bag to spread on top of the arrangement, partly because she likes the background it makes, and partly to give her skin something familiar to touch.

Do you mind? she asks, and is relieved when Danzig says he doesn't. If he has a scene in mind, there's no evidence of it yet.

Assuming he has had as many models here as in the classroom, maybe more, she prefers not to lie where she imagines so many other bodies have rested. For all she knows, this platform has been the stage for countless seductions. She reminds herself, again, that her attraction to Gabe was an exception to her rule, and that she had never before or since repeated it. Lucy had admitted that she thought Danzig was *on the sexy side of town.*

Something about those eyes, Lucy said. He gives off heat.

But that was Lucy.

Don't worry, Merav says to Esther's ghost; I'm safe here. I am perfectly safe.

DANZIG ALWAYS TURNS AWAY to protect the privacy of the model when she dresses and undresses. But it's selfish too: it means he can preserve the first moment of seeing, stay alert to the shape of that initial revelation as it strikes his eye, and not the preparation toward it. As if she exists only in this form for him, not finding her way there.

That's why he has less patience with the models who take poses slowly, as if listening for instructions. He doesn't like telling them what to do. He is interested in his reactions, not in a contrived design. Borrowing from life, rendering.

Merav steps out of her shoes, pulls her sweater over her head, slips out of her skirt in one fluid motion. Nothing more. He isn't watching her; she can feel it, so she has no need to worry about the desire that might be embedded in his gaze.

Standing at his easel, a piece of charcoal already in his hand, Danzig lightly rests his arm on the page, waiting for her to let him know she is ready. When he notices all over again the luminosity of her skin, he is flooded with excitement. And for the first time, he remembers her name.

Merav, he says.

When she turns, he looks at her as if she is entirely new. Let's begin.

IN ONE- AND TWO-MINUTE POSES, Merav leans against the wall, imagining she is listening to neighbors, a song of betrayal and despair.

One hand hovers in the air as if about to begin a piano sonata. Her other arm drapes a hip.

She mimes pinning a wreath of flowers on her head, sits on the edge of a chair and gazes into the dreamy distance while Ella Fitzgerald sings "Autumn in New York."

She tilts her face toward the invisible sun in the high windows, hears a truck rumbling past, its rush of air. Danzig's arm sweeps strokes of darkness onto a white page, bringing the shape of her body into the arc of his virtual embrace. She feels herself translated into charcoal, edged with dust.

For these first twenty minutes, they don't speak at all. Daydreams take Merav traveling, back toward Israel and the life under her skin.

THE ARMY WAS THE PLACE where Merav learned how to see and not be seen, how to explore beneath the desert's surface even as she studied the secrets of camouflage and invisibility. Seeing was both a skill and a trick. The way the desert could look so much like the body and yet be so alien, so difficult for the body to endure. The way constellations and the Milky Way could be the map of the night sky and guide her.

Water in the oasis, Rachel at the well. The lush surprise of palms, figs. Hidden like her secret self.

Secrets were the blessing and the curse of being an only child. Her mother's attitudes veered between obsession and indifference, with periods of obsession offering their own variations of obsessive criticism and obsessive adulation. Thus Merav's sense of her self was volatile, uncertain. She felt on the verge of perfection and hopelessness, the ideal and the disastrous. She was either the center of attention or invisible to the point of annihilation. Nothing, it seemed, could locate her in the realm between those extremes. All seen or all unseen, dimensionally central or utterly vanished.

Sometimes Merav wondered whether Esther had been as confusing a mother as Ilana was. Inviting her daughter to revel in her praise even as she was dismissed. The gaze deflected, brought close and pulled away.

So, Merav undressed to stand naked in front of strangers, offering herself not only for the interpretive power of their gaze but to remind herself that she existed at all.

With Gabe, she had often been a woman with two bodies: one she loved and one she hated. He became her critic, the voice of her mother all over again. He knew when she was expecting her period, commenting on the little extra that bloomed each month around her waist.

It's just water, she told him.

I can always tell, he said.

After leaving him she would stand before the mirror and think hard about loving herself. She thought that if she tried hard enough, her body could become beautiful right before her eyes, shifting shape. Except that she knew she wouldn't be changing at all on the outside; it would be her gaze that was shifting. She would be looking at herself with compassion. With love. As if seeing herself through someone else's eyes, someone full of appreciation and forgiveness. Without judgment or criticism or blame.

WHEN MERAV SAYS it's almost time for her first break, Danzig looks up as if returning to earth from a long orbit. He blinks and squints and frowns.

I want you in this pose again later, he says. These are his first words since she began working. He takes a sip of his coffee and makes a face at its temperature, its sour taste. Merav waits.

I'll mark you, Danzig says, grabbing a roll of masking tape and ripping a few small pieces, placing them at strategic points by Merav's feet, the point where her shoulder touches the wall. His shirt brushes against her arm. Here's where I get paint on me too, she thinks. But nothing appears. All the paint is dry. He's only been working with charcoal.

Okay, he says.

Merav unfolds herself like origami in reverse, one slow limb at a time. Unwinding her head, then one arm, its fingers, the unbending knee. Untwisting her torso. She has memorized the construction so she will find this again, her body in this precise design.

When she pulls her clothing back on, she considers stepping outside for a few moments. The wind appears to be yanking hard on the high branches of the pine trees, roughing them up.

Are you doing all right? Danzig asks. Running one hand

through his hair, making it stick out in several directions, he feels like an out-of-shape athlete rediscovering his muscles.

I'm fine, she says. With his hair like that, he looks a little like the pine trees caught in wild weather, Merav thinks. She stretches herself a little, working the blood back into her arms and legs. The heater has kept her surprisingly warm, considering how much cool space there is all around. Danzig shakes his arms too.

Merav reaches into her bag for a small juice bottle she's brought along. When Danzig opens the barn door he lets the wind push its way inside. She asks him where she can use a bathroom, and he leads her outside along a short path toward the nearby house, which is smaller than the barn and almost as spare. A couch, a handful of chairs, several bookcases piled with oversized art books.

On two walls there are window-sized canvases covered entirely in white. Somehow, colorless, they manage to fill the room with vibration, though at the same time everything seems very still, as if someone had lived there and then abandoned that life.

Danzig points down the hallway and then heads into the kitchen, muttering something about being hungry. In the bathroom, Merav inhales, drawing into herself the sharp medicinal smell of eucalyptus. Everything is neat and precise—cleaned often, she supposes. It's one of those stereotypes, but she can't help it, and she smiles. The studio must be where he wrestles to break loose, the mess finding its way out of form. Order into chaos.

By the time she returns to the barn, Danzig is back at his easel, sorting through the piles of drawings that he tossed to the floor during her first series of poses, wondering if there's anything worth saving. In many of his sketches, he notices Merav's slightly too-wide mouth, the eyes set far enough apart to remind him of the kinds of animals who need extra peripheral vision so they can be ever vigilant to predators.

Yet she has no appearance of the fear he remembers from her poses in his classroom. The drawings tell him that it's not watchfulness but dreaminess in her face, as if she's attending to some inner music even when she looks right at him. Though she doesn't quite do that, he knows. She doesn't look right at him.

He is frustrated, and a groan comes out of him, a sound he doesn't even hear himself making. Something about dissatisfaction with the line, unhappiness with lines in general. He wants less control, even after working with his left hand and making it all so much less perfect. He aches with a desire, a fever, to break every old habit, to force himself toward something new.

DANZIG STOPPED COUNTING the days and weeks he sat or stood or paced beside his easel and waited for something that never came. Often he felt as if he were listening for a sound or a voice without knowing its direction or even its name. The music was always turned off on those days, because none of it felt like exactly the right mood, and all it took was one note from a saxophone to make him irritated or disturbed. Silence was the only thing he could stand, and yet even silence made him grind his teeth and fling gesso at the walls.

The canvas waited for him to decide what to do with it, how to change it into something else. He felt the brutal white of it cutting into him, a kind of knife on the flesh, a

sound like paper being torn between his teeth. An accusation? An invitation? The familiar enemy, beckoning and pro-
voking. What will it be this time? When will you feel ready
to begin again?

Begin again. How many times had he said it? The phrase
that was half encouragement, half admonishment, the con-
stant reminder to his students that beginning was all that
mattered and, at the same time, the very thing that had to be
executed with abandon. Perfect and irrelevant.

He used to turn his paintings to the wall each night so he
could look at them with fresh eyes every morning. But then
he started turning the blank ones away too, as if maybe they
would surprise him with suggestions of color, shape, line.
Now he hangs only those primed canvases on his living room
walls, blinding himself with whiteness, erasing everything
that came before, all his failures and his successes.

SOMETIMES, in his desperation to escape the despair of being
so stifled, he tells himself that these surfaces are enough, a
form of completion, a Zen exercise even though he doesn't
believe in that sort of thing, not really. Though he is in-
trigued by an image of emptiness, the receiving bowl held
out in the beggar's hands, without longing or expectation.
Simply open, held out.

Meanwhile, with their backs turned, the twenty-four canvases stretched tight on frames, covered in zinc white, are
waiting. Prepared for the arrival of an unknown guest, waiting in the dark. They are perfectly ready, his surfaces, and yet
he hasn't been able to touch them.

Nothing has pleased him for such a long time now, not his

own imagination and not the light beyond the windows that used to astonish him without end every morning. Everything feels redundant and unexceptional, offering no reason to capture or preserve or illuminate.

Until this. Until Merav, who seems to bring him back to the revelations of skin, hips, what a face looks like when held in the palm of her hand, the simple beauty of an elbow denting a pillow, the shadow cast by a breast on the soft screen of her own arm. Chin, thigh, kneecap, wrist bone.

If only he could find his way back to paint. He has an impression of himself working thickly, with the palette knife instead of the brush, with his fingers, with sticks. Scraping and erasing, covering over and rediscovering. Concealing in order to reveal. Revealing as a way of distraction from what is concealed, what is withheld. The empty space at the center.

He is still waiting for something, and when he finds it he will know. The colors, the brushstrokes, the shapes and absences: all of that will come too, he hopes, in time.

After pouring some ink into a pan, he gathers some sticks and rags and brushes into a pile by the side of his easel. He will splash this darkness onto the paper, lose the line and find something else. He will.

MERAV SEES that on a small cast-iron table, Danzig has laid out a plate of oranges, bread and cheese, a bottle of red wine, opened, with two glasses.

Help yourself, he says.

She likes the way it resembles a classical still life, something from Cézanne perhaps. It would be nice to pose beside

it, an orange in one hand, its peel drifting toward the floor in
a lazy spiral of brightness. She thinks of Gabe's black-and-
white images, the way she sometimes longed for a dazzle of
vividness to enter and transform them. The starkness of
their apartment had always felt to her so limiting, as if her
own coloring was bleached out when she entered its rooms.

Now she stands considering the wine, the bread and
cheese, its implication of a shared meal. Wine during the day
makes her sleepy, makes her limbs feel as though they belong
to someone else. She loves that feeling at night, as if the
darkness gives her permission to be more loose.

Maybe later, she says.

Danzig is turning on some music while Merav finds the
pose from before. She starts by locating her feet inside the lines
of tape, that homicidal outline, and then feels her way back to
the rest, leaning like an odalisque on a throne of cushions.

The fog must be gone because the light seems stronger
now, though it still pours indirectly through the high windows. Yo-Yo Ma begins playing Bach cello suites again. Descending scales and ascending light. Merav feels the heater
trying to reach across her skin.

She wonders what they are hiding, those canvases with
their faces to the walls, and she realizes that in this pose she
has her back turned too. She's not partly turned away but
turned all the way around, not glancing over her shoulder
even.

Maybe later she will turn toward him, and they will stay
with one another, gaze on gaze. But not yet.

She hears the scratchy sound of a stick on a white page.
She hears the cello full of longing and memory. Maybe

Danzig is searching for the light, finding it on her shoulder, in a triangle across her rib cage. The cello traces outlines, traces her thoughts flying up toward the high windows.

Tell me about your boyfriend, Danzig says.

He is assuming of course that she has one, or maybe even more than one, with a face like that, mood coming through like headlights cutting through fog. Something about her makes him want to keep her there all day and night, so he can keep feeling this way: a renewal of determination, or faith maybe, as if something inside him is struggling to be born and he has to be patient beyond his own limits.

He has to be willing to dig into the darkest earth as if there is some forgotten village buried under earthquake rubble after all the survivors are dead for generations.

I don't have one, Merav says.

Danzig makes a sound that indicates his surprise.

Married? he says.

Merav suddenly wishes she had her uniform nearby, even a costume to step into so that Danzig would see the soldier in her. But she left her uniform in Israel with her mother to prevent herself from tearing it into pieces, using strips of it for rags, or maybe even burning it in a kind of ritual. She had wanted some way to demystify it, treat it like the dull green fabric it was instead of a symbol of power and violence and offensive defense or whatever could be said about that way of life she had tried to leave so far behind.

I was married for a while, she says. To a photographer.

Danzig snorts at the idea. They always want to put frames around things, he says. They pretend they're only telling you what they claim is out there in so-called real life, but really they're getting in the way just as much as painters are.

At first, Merav doesn't say anything, doesn't agree or disagree. Then she says, He is color-blind.

Danzig says Ha! as if something has been proved in support of his case. He has always thought of photographs as lies, as mechanical reproductions of some fleeting moment that has no mood or meaning except the one imposed by the camera, and he tells her so.

He said he dreams in red light, Merav says.

Danzig doesn't comment, but this strange fact about her ex-husband hangs in the air like the smell of something burning. Susan's face appears out of nowhere, the red imprint of his hand on her cheek. And then he sees Andrea with hands on her belly, hating him. He wonders whether Merav is living with some equally bitter memories of her life with the photographer, whether she too has to suffer what Danzig knows about love going wrong.

Merav is startled to realize that what she really wants to talk about is Yossi. Because he was the one who should have been her husband. He always speaks in the language of her dreams, the one who floats beside her every time she swims.

She would put all the pieces back together if she could.

Danzig sighs audibly. Merav keeps these thoughts of Yossi to herself. Bach measures the silence between them.

BEFORE DRIVING OUT to Point Reyes, Merav had extracted a map of Marin county from her pile, her fingers tracing the wide contours of its open space. Now she would have another piece of landscape to add to her inner geography, a stretch beyond the Muir redwoods and the curves of the coastal highways.

For years while Merav collected maps she knew she was waiting for some reason to come clear: why she thought of them like another kind of clothing, the way the land and all of her life rested on the surface of things. When she was living with Gabe, she saw how carefully and minutely he studied the outer world, and wondered whether all she needed to know was taking place right there before her eyes.

Somehow she was never convinced. Her modeling was about the body, and yet the true source of her work was what lived inside, inescapable and invisible. Hers was the art of remaining present even as she disappeared. Inhabiting her body and dreaming her way out of it.

In the army, she spent months reading topographical maps, reading the mysterious and compelling vocabulary of sand. Even now, the heat lived deep in her bones. She spent weeks hiking in the Sinai, meeting up with camel drivers at night who cooked tea under a sky densely splashed with the Milky Way.

With three other soldiers, Merav sat beside a Bedouin's fire, listening to him speak about the desert, its patterns of sun and wind. The camels stood near them in the dark, shifting their weight. She loved their movements, the way they knelt to receive the burden of their packs, the layers of carpet and leather spread across their humps.

Over and over, she remembered lying with Yossi, unable to sleep under that glittering sky because the stars filled her with too much delight.

DANZIG HUMS, mumbles words Merav can't make out. It's as if he is having some kind of private conference, perhaps a debate. She counts time in her heart, the way she usually does for short poses, but this time it's to measure her breathing, match it to the music. She is the space between movements. There's a deep breath for the cellist, for the cello, the audience, the strings. Then the wooden body resting from its vibrations.

Seven more minutes, she says.

From the corner of her eye she sees the embroidered bag she uses for the modeling payments, the piece of fabric given to her by that nomadic Bedouin, woven with scents of the desert. She thinks of it as her trading bag, the money an exchange for her performance as a belly dancer who doesn't dance except inside the tent of someone else's imagination.

Aware and trying to ignore it, she feels Danzig's hunger reaching toward her. Those boundless desires, the artists who want more and more of her. For a long time she thought it was up to her to satisfy them, as if feeding a banquet, endlessly serving up pieces of herself until there was nothing left.

Gabe, hovering with his camera, tried to find out what she held reflected in her pupils, and of course found only himself there, that mirror. He wanted to use her in order to say, Look at this, I made this. To put himself inside the frame without actually being visible but to be the one holding the frame. To imply himself even as he pretended to stay out of it. The illusion of seeing, getting so close that all the edges disappeared.

As if the difference between inside and outside could be erased that easily. As if physical distance has anything to do with intimacy, with connecting.

Time, she says.

MOMENTS LATER, they are standing outside the barn, breathing deeply into the fresh air, and Merav is temporarily back inside her sweater and skirt, her outer layer. The wind blows her hair into her face and out again, strands getting caught at the edges of her mouth. Danzig wants to touch her at least this much, to push the hair back behind one of her ears. But he doesn't.

There is something he needs to say out loud, something that can't remain unsaid, even as he fears he is risking everything.

You know I'm German, don't you.

Merav hesitates, but nods with her head down. And then, for the first time, she raises her face and holds his gaze without looking away. His eyes look like the blue of an oasis. Water buried among rocks, blazing sun all around.

I know, she says.

And you're an Israeli, he says.

He holds out a hand that is empty of brushes, his fingers deeply stained with ink, black under the short fingernails. The gesture hangs in the air. Both of them look at the palm of his hand, the way the charcoal residue has collected in the deep creases, his riverbed of lifelines.

I didn't know whether you knew or not, she says.

Of course I knew, the first time you spoke, just as you did with me.

They are wordless again. It would be a moment for pulling deeply on a cigarette if either of them smoked. Merav imagines there is smoke in the air anyway, but of course it's just the remnants of the morning fog still burning off.

I was born after the war, Danzig says, and allows himself the long release of a sigh. There's a name for us, he says. *Nachgeborenen.* The ones born after.

Merav doesn't reply right away. The ones born after. The ones never born.

She thinks of the Mercedes all over Israel, the buses and taxicabs, that symbol adorning every hood. It was one of those haunting paradoxes: Germany's reparations in the form of a circle of metal, every vehicle saying We're Sorry. There is no question of forgiveness, Merav thinks.

Danzig clears his throat as if to say something else, but he can't seem to speak, not with her standing there like that.

Merav almost says, My grandmother, but she stops herself. Does telling Danzig about Esther make any sense? Is he supposed to be ashamed? They stand there, looking at each other and looking away. She imagines she can feel the weight of it on him, the burdens of his own history.

Israelis often travel to Germany, she says. As if they have to see something in order to make sense of anything. Or maybe they are trying to prove they exist, prove they are fighting back. I don't know. I never went.

I haven't lived there since I was twenty, Danzig says. And I won't go back.

She doesn't say it, but she is thinking about how she was Born After too, even longer afterwards than he had been. Every year of her life in Israel she had stood inside that two minutes of silence, remembering, being alive along with the rest of them.

Here we are, she says. Not in either of our countries but somewhere else. Someplace we chose.

182

He crosses his hands over his chest, not in defiance but as if to shield himself. You mean you don't want to kill me? he says. He attempts something like a smile but it is more of a grimace. There was a time in my life I would have thought you had a right.

Merav believes that these aren't questions to be answered. She won't ask any of her own either. The ones that he's probably expecting. What about the ones who brought you into the world. Where were they. What did they do.

Would she want to know?

He is a painter. She is his model.

They are making something together. Everything they both carry, everything they both left behind. She doesn't touch him, although she considers it. A hand on his shoulder. But it's not necessary. They are standing close enough already.

Let's go back to work, he says.

MERAV TAKES A MEDITATIVE WALK around the inside of the studio, slowing herself down while Danzig pours himself a glass of wine. She heads toward the dimmest corner where the sheet-draped bathtub sits, and lifts up one of the corners. Is this what I think it is? she says.

Came with the barn, Danzig says. Not connected to anything.

Too bad, she says, mostly to herself, wishing she could fill it with water. She imagines walking back and forth between the house and the studio carrying a full jug on her head, one hand up to steady its weight, the other hand casual, dangling, and her swaying hips the eternal female body in motion. In

the warm water she would pose like a nymph with one ear
submerged, the side of her face resting as if on a pillow.

This is how she imagines it, climbing in and out, dipping
one foot as if to test the temperature, reaching for an invisible towel to dry off. She pictures herself dripping, rising like
a shipwreck, an apparition, one of Gabe's photographs emerging from its chemical bath and coming to life.

On the kibbutz, there was a pool where Merav learned to
swim. A young man from South Africa with a wonderfully
smooth chest and a melodious accent taught her how it was
possible to surrender to the buoyancy while at the same time
mastering it. She loved the paradox of it all, especially the feeling of freedom she discovered underwater, as if she had found
her true self at last, a creature of the water instead of the land.

Even now she often fantasizes about living submerged. As
a child she practiced holding her breath longer and longer,
delighting in the way time slowed down when she could
spend it deep beneath the surface. Underwater she could listen inside herself, her drumming pulse. She dreamed sometimes that she could breathe underwater, dreamed of staying
down there for days at a time.

But always the pressure in her lungs would eventually
force her, gasping, to the surface, until she learned how to
control even that moment so she'd emerge quietly, pull the
air into her lungs in a way that revealed to no one just how
desperately she needed it. She was simply another creature
rising up to study what lay beyond her liquid world: the sky
and its endless variation of clouds, the eucalyptus trees that
encircled the clearing where the pool had been built, the
rows of chairs and tables and umbrellas. The other people,

the ones on dry land, seemed to her to be strangers from another country.

These days, in the locker rooms of the public pools and in her own bathroom, she studies herself in the mirror. She longs to look through her own softened heart and see her imperfections as perfect. Her cello hips and small breasts, the ones that can disappear completely behind her cupped hands. If she could truly see herself the way her clients see her, maybe then she would finally and forever be at peace with her body. Not the one she imagines herself to possess but the one she owns, the one she keeps offering up to everyone else.

Once a painter who was also a masseuse offered to do a weekly trade with her, a two-hour massage in exchange for two hours of modeling. The bargain seemed irresistible. Christina had said she could teach Merav where her tendons joined to the bone, teach her to feel her very own anatomy. It almost seemed like a continuation of her drawing lessons from Tel Aviv, years ago. The truth of the body, its knots and unravelings, its secrets of release.

Merav learned by way of Christina's hands how she was made, how to remember the long muscles of her thighs, the way her shoulder blades conceal and protect the puzzle of her heart, her lungs. Merav breathed into the pain as Christina worked her fingers into her; she told herself these aches were just neutral sensations like any other, a message her brain could accept without judgment.

Skin, tendon, bone. She is all of that and none of it. She is somewhere in the spot between her eyes, listening and watching. Inside out and outside in. Underneath.

I'VE GOT AN IDEA, Danzig says.

He pushes open the barn door and comes back a minute later with an old bicycle, its wide handlebars and fat wheels leading the way. He is raising his eyebrows at her in a challenge.

How about a ride, he says.

There is, in fact, plenty of room. Danzig turns up the music full blast and the sound fills the barn. Beatles, Rolling Stones. The songs seem to be all about letting go, riding the air with abandon.

After giving it a quick wipe with a cloth, Merav climbs onto the worn leather seat for her first-ever naked ride. Soon she begins moving in wide looping circles, feeling her way into harmony with the bike's gravity and balance. She takes one hand at a time off the handlebars, experimenting with shape and line, feeling that strange blend of deliberation and surprise, an ageless child.

The music makes her want to dance too, and when she gets tired of circling around, she leans the rusty frame against a crate.

Danzig says, All right, do whatever you want, just keep moving.

He is working with the ink in big arm movements that mimic what Merav was doing on the bike. She heads toward the dark corner of the barn and pulls the sheet from the bathtub, using it like a giant cape, moving like one of Isadora Duncan's dancers. Merav dances until she feels too tired to go on, and then she arranges the sheet inside the bathtub, no longer questioning her impulses.

She climbs in and settles herself onto the folded cotton,

thinking of Bonnard's nudes. His incessant depictions of
Marthe, wife and muse, eternally on her way into and out of
the bath, all of that orange and lavender splashed across her
skin.

Danzig, on the far side of the studio, watches her. He
barely notices that the music has stopped, and he doesn't
move to start it again. She is closing her eyes, loosening
toward sleep. Slowly, quietly, he approaches the tub, not
wanting to startle her, sensing the heaviness of her limbs as
she surrenders. Her lips part, her fingers twitch briefly, and
her eyelids flutter with dream life. He holds his breath, waiting.

WHEN SHE AWAKENS, Merav sees that the light has changed
from a kind of matte gray to a softer and translucent peach,
filtering now through more layers of matter and pollution in
the air, turning her skin a soft gold.

Danzig has moved his easel closer to the tub; he has been
drawing her in her sleep. She says, How long was I gone?

Just long enough, he says, touching the pages in front of
him.

The bicycle leans against a crate with a stenciled label
reading CHINA, and Merav imagines herself climbing inside
that box, making a nest that would keep her safe and comfortable for the long voyage to the other side of the world.
Looking over at the still life of bread, cheese, and oranges,
she pictures herself gathering those things and bringing
them into the crate: supplies for the journey.

Are you thirsty? Danzig says, handing her an orange.
Merav, still reclining, accepts it into her open palm and then

slowly peels the skin away from the flesh. She watches the membranes pull apart and send particles of liquid and fragrance into the air.

A long time ago, Danzig says, one of my students told me a story about a rice farmer in Vietnam who escaped to America. Boat people, remember? His only provisions for the small fishing boat were seven oranges. He couldn't imagine that the size of the ocean he was crossing could be any more than seven oranges' worth of distance.

Did he survive? Merav asks.

After he told me the story, my student told me that the farmer was his father, Danzig says. It was his father's voyage.

She tears one section at a time and holds the juice in her mouth, as if to quench the thirst of a rice farmer in exile. He was farther from land than he'd ever been, with no shore in sight, only the wind and the waves for company. And of course, more than anything the taste of the orange reminds her of the kibbutz orchard, of fruit picked right off the trees. The memory is so sweet that it makes her mouth ache.

What do you miss from your home? Danzig says. He has gone over to start the music up again.

The obvious and most true answer is Yossi, but she still can't bring herself to mention his name out loud. Oranges, she says, taking another slow-motion bite. She is reluctant to ask Danzig his own question, isn't sure she wants to know what he might be missing. He said he would never go back, but that could be true for the rice farmer too. Oceans crossed and left behind.

Can I leave the bathtub yet? Merav asks.

Danzig is gazing at his shelves of brushes as if he might will them to life in his hands. Not yet, he says. Please.

He stretches an arm toward one of the jars, and then another, gathering brushes into an embrace with his paint-splattered shirt. The nearby sink is stained with a hundred shades of color.

He hums in harmony with the voice of Van Morrison. Merav thinks they sound good together.

The strange thing is how much, when she really thinks about it, Danzig reminds her of Tzvi on the kibbutz. He was the only one who dared to make art his contribution to the collective, his huge wall-sized canvases, abstractions that took him months at a time to work on. She remembers that he spent entire days in a chair facing the canvas, never once applying a single brushstroke of color. As if he were waiting for instructions.

Tzvi was the one who told Merav that the word "muse" came from the word "mouth." She would bring him tea sometimes, or a bowl of fruit, something to place near his lips and to relieve him of the hours of waiting. How did he know whether or not something, eventually, would come?

All of this is spinning in Merav's head as Danzig hums and arranges his brushes. Suddenly he goes back to his easel, squatting and sifting through the loose pages he has scattered on the floor. Some of the sketches have notes on them in a kind of hieroglyphic arrangement, notes for some future composition.

Danzig runs one hand through his hair, a gesture Merav already recognizes as habitual; he rubs at his jaw and his forehead.

Asleep, she had made it all so clear. For the first long minutes, he had been able to look only at her hand, the one that dangled on the edge of the bathtub, catching light and reflecting it back, the shiny porcelain gleaming like an enormous set of teeth. He stared at her hand until the colors came back to him, impossible to forget: the grays of the sky before a storm, the unearthly blues.

Before he can question it, he is squeezing color onto a palette, dipping the tip of the smallest brush into the pool. Please, he says.

AND SO IT HAPPENS: the cracking open, when Danzig knows with perfect certainty that he is ready. Instead of reaching for her with his body, he understands with the force of a revelation that he can use his brush to do that. He can paint Merav's body as the step he has to take toward the canvas, for the canvas will be her skin.

He thinks of all the times he scraped at old paintings to undo, erase, and destroy. There were so many times he had to say good-bye to everything from before, reminding himself that nothing was permanent, nothing complete. It was like music sometimes, the notes piling on top of one another, enthusiastic and abundant, pouring into a riot of sound. What would emerge on the canvas was a pastiche of half-formed shapes, ghost images, pigments leaking through where he'd only partially scraped them away. The history of decision.

A cubist underpainting would keep weaving its way into the new painting. A window in the corner, a glimpse of infinity. There by accident, a remnant of an old vision even though no window had been there before.

Glazing could do that too, enable him to work back into a painting, build in shadows and tones and pull them back again. He worked with a mixture of linseed oil and varnish and turpentine, or the premixed Liquin, or that other mixture so combustible he'd always heard that the man who makes it does the mixing with his arms wrapped around a tree trunk in case it all explodes.

And of course Danzig has felt that way himself sometimes: that the act of creating keeps him on the verge of exploding.

The dark glazing colors are the ones that look black in the tube, glossy and deep. He knows how to spread them like a stain, like the sudden blotting out of sunlight, like a bad mood. He could unify a whole piece, or rub it away with a rag to bring back some areas of brightness. He could work with paint again, coming back for more color, more intensity.

"How many times?" they'd asked Velasquez, and he'd said, "Forty. Until it's enough, until it lets you go."

He wants that trance now. His mind disengaging, his eyes tuned to color, shape, relationship. He wants to mix paint, squeeze life from a tube, dip his brushes and bring them up full. Now as if conjuring both his former selves and the self he's about to become, he holds his brushes, each carrying some old story and yet together forming a gesture of anticipation. One color at a time and all at once. Color as his vocabulary of light.

In all those years of making abstract paintings embedded in each inch of the canvas, even when he was working in realistic mode, what he needed to see and believe in was the movement of paint in any given patch, textures and collisions and miracles. Making order out of chaos, even when he was the one creating the chaos in the first place. Remembering that color is always about light, the juxtapositions that make the colors vibrate. Like chords. Like bodies.

MERAV DOESN'T QUITE KNOW what she's agreeing to, at first. Danzig barely seems to know how to explain what he's asking for, except that against all expectation she is willing to trust him. Using the microwave to heat some paints, he arranges a handful of jars so full of color they promise to glow in the dark. And suddenly he is standing before her, the warmed acrylics all arrayed and gleaming, and with his softest brushes offered up like a bouquet.

For me? she says.

Sort of, he says. All you have to do is keep the faith. And then he laughs at himself.

Faith? asks Merav.

Or something, he says, knowing that what he really means is Trust me. You get to be landscape and figure all at once, he says. A temporary masterpiece.

Everything's temporary, she says.

MERAV IS BEING MADE BLANK, an uncreated surface. Caressing her pale skin, the brushes in Danzig's hands begin to glaze her even paler to pure white, from the line of her jaw in long strokes downward, pulling like gravity toward her toes. She feels the gentle touch of the bristles, the warm paint, the air from the heater pulsing toward her, a whisper of something that must be Danzig's breath as he moves above and around her.

She keeps her eyes closed, as if this is something she is dreaming. It amazes her to realize that she had fallen asleep in front of him, had managed to trust him enough for that. To have forgotten every possible danger in his presence, as if her body knew he was not an enemy. And now, almost being touched, her skin can still belong to her even as she surrenders to this momentary possession, even as she allows him to borrow her for these hours.

She thinks of her time in the desert, training, waiting for the heat to fade, waiting for the sun to drop far enough below the horizon for the sand to be cool enough to be bearable. She and Talia exchanged stories of dehydration and madness, their shared fears of dying of thirst. Not just an expression, some melodramatic prediction, but an actual possibility, the thin line between preparation and catastrophe.

Gabe used to sleep with his arm over his forehead as if to block a bright glare. The other arm dangled off the edge of the mattress, which they kept on the floor. A mirror propped behind the bed was their headboard, the place where Gabe used to fix his gaze while they made love. He was so intent, and so blind. His camera got this close, as close as Danzig was getting now, except that it was too close, and he wasn't seeing her. She was disappearing before his eyes, a mirage, her skin like the dried riverbeds and cracked earth of her beloved desert, hiding the crevasses where the water is held.

DANZIG WORKS SLOWLY, attending to everything convex and concave, smooth and rough. Leaving her face exposed, he makes Merav look like a Greek statue coming to life or a woman turning to stone. She could be yet another of his prepared canvases, reproaching him, but this time he's not turning away.

As the white paint dries, Danzig rinses brushes, tests the colors to ensure they are viscous enough to adhere but fluid enough to follow the curves of Merav's legs and hips and breasts and shoulders. All the blues he can find. Ultramarine. Sapphire. Indigo. Periwinkle. Azure.

Every inch of her becomes his own invention.

And here is what's astonishing: not for a single moment does he wish he were using his hands or his tongue to explore her. This is so much more than enough.

LATER, AFTER DANZIG is collapsed in a chair and breathing so rhythmically he sounds asleep, Merav will begin to move. First her fingers and toes make small waving motions like a sea anemone whose tentacles have been brushed by a wave. Then there is a rippling upward and outward, her chest filling with air, her body unfolding from its suspension.

She climbs out of the tub, pulling the sheet with her, smearing it with paint. Her skin releases what it can and holds on to the rest; soon it looks as if a battle has been fought, a wrestling with demons or angels or both. An accidental painting is being made even now.

Danzig isn't asleep, of course, and he watches Merav undoing his work, returning to the creature that is utterly separate from him. The messages of bone and ligament, the cavities and joints, the elevations and interpretations he has touched with his brush, has claimed for a moment. They belong to her alone now.

What makes the right amount of flesh to cover and expose, conceal and reveal? What makes some people more beautiful inside clothing, while others are at their best unclothed? Merav is clearly of the second kind, the kind whose life unveiled is irresistibly beautiful. Astonishing.

He desperately wishes he could watch her bathe in the tub, watch her rinse herself and turn the clear water into an ocean. Somehow that huge piece of porcelain dangling like heartbreak in the bombed apartment building—somehow that, along with finding Margot, has merged into one echo, one story. All of that past is being painted over, transformed.

Margot's was the first naked female body he ever saw, or at least the first one he remembered seeing.

He inhales sharply, remembering.

She took her life.

Such a strange expression. As if she might have taken another but chose her own. Except that what is meant is that she left. She took herself away.

AND ART DISAPPEARS TOO, just like this: Merav in motion, the paint smudging and unraveling. The way he'd made his paintings of Susan disappear, as if doing that would erase his memories of her too, because that wild-eyed look of hers still haunted him and he wanted it gone. He wanted it never to have happened.

But he also wanted the death of his sister never to have happened, and once you started unraveling there was no end to it. Loose threads everywhere, all the way to the beginning.

What about his own birth, for that matter, given where he came from and who brought him into being? A mother allowing herself to be impregnated by a monster, even if she pretended to herself he was a decent man, worthy all over again of fatherhood, in spite of everything. Maybe she even thought it might redeem them to create something new, to start over.

Was his own life the new canvas his parents wanted a chance to paint? Or was he giving them too much credit? They just wanted another chance to have a son; maybe that was all.

Margot took her life. She left no note. A stone dropped into a well and never hitting water, never echoing back its arrival.

DON'T LEAVE YET, he says to Merav. Please.

She sees Danzig in the chair, looks at the white sheet smeared with paint, her own skin a palette. Sidewalk paintings turning to rivers of color in the rain.

I need to shower, she says.

It's not toxic, he says.

I know. But I want my skin back.

Go inside, he says. It's all right. Take as long as you want. There's plenty of hot water. And a scrub brush.

All right.

You look like the sea, he says. All those blues.

She laughs. And back to the sea I will go. She wipes the soles of her feet on the sheet so she won't make footprints in the house.

The music has stopped. It's so quiet she can hear the wind.

IN THE SHOWER, the paints blur with soap and sluicing water, all of it cascading down her legs and pooling at her feet before swirling down the drain. From the window she can see a sliver of Tomales Bay, wind-whipped and turbulent, with the

Pacific stretching invisibly in the distance. She is so far from her arid origins.

Studying her hands in the shower, she pictures herself in the days when she first learned to hold a gun, fitting her fingers to its steel curves, learning its weight and balance. Such a strange history, from planting trees to milking cows to shooting bullets.

Will the sound of that explosion last longer in her head than any other music?

At home, in her studio, a pile of maps has been waiting for her, and on one wall, a gift from Arlene in the Monday group: Merav sketched darkly against a background of the Sinai desert, a page torn from an old atlas, in the days before Israel had official statehood, before boundaries and war. There she was, her torso curving across the wide expanses of sand. Her breasts like sand dunes, rising anonymously toward a blank blue sky.

On a table below the wall where the drawing is hanging, Merav has piled maps, the ones she's been collecting all of her life, the ones from her Israeli life and the ones from her American life, all mixed up together. Obsolete and brand-new, waterlogged, torn, unopened. Everything in between. A paper trail dangling from the heels of her bare feet.

Map sculptures, that's what is waiting for her.

Not about audience, about being received, about instructing or changing anything or anyone. Just the story she wants to understand, the pieces that never quite fit together and yet somehow need to be made whole: her grandmother's exile, her missing father, her migration to another country and a reinvented self. The fragments of Yossi buried in the ground. The maps of what is missing.

Always the landscape wanting to touch at the edges, the lines persisting beneath oceans of distance, the connections that still connect.

Even with Yossi dead, or maybe especially with Yossi dead, the pull toward and away from Israel lives in her body, even now. She thinks of the families who quietly and daily practice the art of survival, their children riding on different buses and no one ever speaking the reason out loud: if one is hit they won't all die together.

And Merav said No, I will not live like this anymore because it seems we are all turned into murderers, one way or another, because we want in our hearts for the dead to be from someone else's home and someone else's country.

Wrapped in one of Danzig's clean towels, she is struck by the idea of Yossi's wedding, the groom he never was. He would have been wrapped in a tallis, the only time she might have ever seen him in anything remotely religious. And he would have stepped on the glass, making everything shatter.

All the way here in California, she recalls the sound of his laughter, his army boots on the front step of his little bungalow that let her know he was back on the kibbutz for the weekend. He was the first one who really looked at her, suddenly one day transforming from a sweet older brother to a desire-filled young man. And she had felt his gaze like a flame.

More and more comes flooding back to her: the way the air smelled early in the morning when the sprinklers were on and the earth's perfumes rose like a scent from a lover's body. The way people greeted one another in the predawn darkness on their way to work: a very low murmuring sound because it wasn't really morning yet and the words for good morning seemed premature.

The stars, the moon, the sound of the truck engines to take them into the fields. Yossi driving the truck, and Merav getting to sit up front with him, and the lovely thick silence between them.

Islands in reverse. Israel as an island in a sea of enemies, the eternal story, narrated by the heroes who keep surviving. Merav has left it behind even as she recognizes she will always carry its echo within her, not escaping it completely. And yet she keeps trying, struggling to transcend or at least coexist with an equally powerful idea of life as hopeful and whole.

She does not want to live as if about to be annihilated. She will not accept that as the truth.

BACK IN THE BARN, Merav stands with a turban around her wet hair and another towel around her body. She goes over to the heater for a moment before reaching for her clothes, and Danzig smiles at her.

I'd hold you for more warmth, he says, but I won't.

Merav nods. Right, she says.

We don't even have to discuss it, he says.

Good.

I'm actually getting this, he says. He laughs. I mean, it almost makes sense. Except you're so beautiful.

And we're not even going to discuss it, Merav says.

Right, says Danzig, laughing. Right.

All these years of longing to be seen, the push and pull of all those eyes. Where is the gaze that will find her all the way beneath her bones? Not Gabe and not here, not Danzig. Not any of them.

Herself. Her own gaze.

The maps she contains are like the ones monarch butter-flies know, and migrating birds. The ones that don't get memorized but are simply carried in some coded message deep in the DNA, the way the desert baked its heat into her bones.

She will go back to her studio and lie on the floor, maps spread out like blankets. She will stretch herself so that fin-gertips at the Atlantic reach away from toes at the Pacific. And the equator will bisect her, an imaginary ribbon wrap-ping around her rib cage, her belly in the southern hemi-sphere and her breasts to the north.

She will remake the world. Cut the maps and stitch them back together in a design of peace. She will stretch them around chicken wire, glue them onto wood, make bowls of papier-mâché. She will rebuild the globes of her childhood, except that this time the oceans will be vaster than ever, countries reduced to small islands half submerged. In a high tide entire cities could vanish, at least for a while.

She will stretch the blues even wider, washing sea water over everything.

AND WHILE MERAV is unwrapping her towels and replacing her clothing, covering up and disappearing, Danzig pulls himself out of his stupor, awake now as if he has been asleep for years.

He wants her, but not in the flesh.

Hoffman was right all along: Danzig needs Merav to leave so that he can work from memory. Abandoned paint-drenched sheets record the path of her rising up and walking away, a perfect blue departure. The ghost of Margot, hovering, can finally be released.

When he holds the brush, paint dripping with life will find its way onto the skin of the canvas. The twenty-four white fields he's been perfecting, waiting with the silence of a garden in winter, the begging of an empty bowl—they are ready at last to be filled.

He will turn them around.

They will face one another, and he will hold a loaded brush in his hand, and he will begin. Again.

Acknowledgments

Special thanks to Lynne Knight, whose poetic sensibilities and wide heart helped reaffirm my path. To Armand Volkas, whose courageous Acts of Reconciliation brought so much discovery of truth. To Daniel Menaker, for the rescue brought by his belief in this book. And for his relentless faith and invaluable guidance, thank you (such small words!) to Dan Smetanka. Some gifts can never be repaid.

ELIZABETH ROSNER's first novel, *The Speed of Light*, debuted on the *San Francisco Chronicle*'s bestseller list at number 2 and has received awards and literary recognition in the United States as well as in Europe. Translated into nine languages, and winner of the inaugural Prix France Bleu Gironde in 2004, *The Speed of Light* was a Book Sense 76 selection, one of Borders' Original Voices, a Hadassah National Book Selection, and the one-city, one-book Peoria Reads! 2004 selection. Ms. Rosner received the prestigious Harold U. Ribalow Prize as well as the Great Lakes Colleges Association prize for new writers of fiction.

She is also an award-winning poet. Her collection *Gravity*, published by Small Poetry Press, is in its thirteenth printing. Her poems and short fiction have been widely published in literary magazines.

Born in Schenectady, New York, she graduated from Stanford University in 1981 and subsequently earned an MFA in fiction from the University of California at Irvine in 1985 and a Master of Literary Studies from the University of Queensland in Australia in 1990. She has lived in California since 1978 and taught creative writing at the college level for twenty years. She now lives and writes in Berkeley.

This book was set in a digital version of Monotype Walbaum. The original typeface was created by Justus Erich Walbaum (1768–1839) in 1810. Before becoming a punch cutter with his own type foundries in Goslar and Weimar, he was apprenticed to a confectioner where he is said to have taught himself engraving, making his own cookie molds using tools made from sword blades. The letterforms were modeled on the "modern" cuts being made at the time by Giambattista Bodoni and the Didot family.